FIELDS' GUIDE TO VOODOO

JULIE MULHERN

J & M Press

Created with Vellum

Acknowledgments

As always, my thanks to my endlessly patient family, to Gretchen who talks me off ledges, and to Rachel, who makes me better than I am.

Chapter One

"You can't fight fate." My college roommate, Adele Coombs, lifted a Pimm's cup to her lips but didn't drink. Instead, she stared at the street below us.

We sat on the veranda at the Columns Hotel at a table covered with a green linen cloth. A gentle breeze cooled our skin. The street below us was St. Charles Avenue, and any minute now, another trolley would roll by. We were supposed to be talking about a week's worth of festivities. I was supposed to make sure that every event was correctly entered into the calendar on my cell. But Adele had turned philosophical. I blamed the gin.

"Sure, you can."

Adele laughed softly. "Maybe you can."

Was she having second thoughts? "Adele, if you're not one hundred percent certain about Carter, don't marry him."

"Oh, I'm sure about Carter." A small smile curled her lips. "Carter and I are fine. It's this—" she side-eyed the tables closest to us, leaned forward, and lowered her voice "—this production is too much."

"Elope."

Her eyes widened as if I'd suggested she run naked down Canal Street. "I'm the first Coombs daughter in four generations. Daddy, my uncles, my aunts—they'd all kill me. Not to mention Momma." She shuddered. "I'm all in on this one, and it has to be perfect."

Adele was right about the expectations settled upon her shoulders. She was also right about the production. The wedding was more than a week away and it seemed as if every minute, right up until the exchange of vows, was spoken for. There were luncheons, and showers, and cocktail parties, and fittings, and a bachelorette spa day. Not to mention the rehearsal dinner and the brunch the day after the wedding. I'd had no idea what I was signing up for when I'd agreed to be a bridesmaid.

"In just over a week you'll be on a beach in St. Bart's."

"You're right. You're right. If I focus on that, I might survive the crazy." Adele sat back in her chair. "I can't believe I'm complaining about crazy to you."

"Hopefully I've got all my crazy out of the way." I'd been kidnapped by a Mexican drug lord, then sucked into a plot to blow up Paris. I'd also been recruited to work for a secret government agency (not that Adele knew about that). While she and Carter were enjoying their honeymoon, I'd be at some sort of spy basic training.

"Tell me about Paris." Adele regarded me with cornflower blue eyes. Those eyes coupled with her blonde hair and tiny frame gave her more than a passing resemblance to a Madame Alexander doll.

"Anything you read in the papers is probably true."

"Your mother saved Sacré-Coeur?"

Not that. But I wasn't about to tell anyone, not even one of my best friends, what had really happened. "Parisians are treating her like she's Wonder Woman. It's officially her favorite city on the planet. She may never leave."

"Chariss in Paris?" She winced at the rhyme. "Doesn't that make your life easier?" Being my roommate, Adele had seen firsthand the challenges of being a movie star's daughter.

"Nothing about Chariss is easy. Ever."

"Seriously, what happ—" She scowled at the phone vibrating on the table. "It's Momma. Do you mind? If I don't answer, she'll just keep calling."

"Go ahead."

Consuela, the Chihuahua who'd adopted me, was curled in my lap. She lifted her sleepy head and yawned.

I scratched behind her ears and gazed past the enormous white columns that gave the hotel its name. Traffic on St. Charles sped by.

While people in New Orleans might take a *laissez-les-bon-temps-rouler* attitude towards drinking, dining, music, and life in general, they drove like maniacs.

Case in point, some lunatic in a Mercedes G-Wagon raced toward us at what had to be a hundred miles per hour.

"What an idiot," I whispered to Consuela.

"*Grrr.*"

The G-Wagon wove through traffic, almost as if it were being pursued. It clipped a bumper, spun out of control, and wrapped itself around a light pole in front of the hotel.

The sound of crunching metal had everyone on the terrace dropping their jaws and jumping out of their chairs.

The G-Wagon's passenger's door opened, and a man staggered out of the car. He was short and stocky, and his face was covered in blood. In his left hand, he clutched a pistol.

Before any of the people on the veranda could do more than gasp, the man lurched toward us.

"Momma, I gotta go." Adele dropped her phone.

In the street, a Range Rover screeched to a stop. Doors flew open and men poured out of the vehicle. Men with guns—guns bigger than a pistol.

"Get down." I pushed Adele and Consuela to the concrete.

And just in time. The man with the pistol dashed up the stairs and into the hotel.

The men pursuing him opened fire.

Bullets whizzed by us, shattering glass, reducing tables to sticks, pocking the hotel's wood siding.

I reached for my handbag and my gun—not that a .22 was much use against six men armed with AR-15s.

Three of the men vaulted onto the veranda, raced past us, and burst through the remains of the front door.

Next to me, Adele raised up on her hands and knees.

"Don't move," I whispered. "Stay down."

"But—"

"Stay down." Hopefully my tone conveyed what a monumentally awful idea drawing attention was.

"*Grrr.*" Consuela agreed with my assessment.

One of the men who'd run into the hotel appeared at the door. "He escaped out the back."

The three men still standing in the lawn raced to the Range Rover, piled in, and sped away.

The man in the doorway swept his gaze over the people cowering on the terrace. Six feet tall, dark hair, brown eyes, a divot in his chin. I'd recognize him again. I lowered my eyes before he caught me staring.

When I looked up a second time, he was gone.

For a few seconds, the silence stretched. Then a woman's cries rose to the ceiling fans still whirring above us.

"We need help. He's hit," a man yelled.

I shifted, relieving the pressure where the concrete pressed into my hip bone. "Are you okay?"

"*Yiiiip!*" Consuela was okay, and she was pissed.

Adele's eyes were the size of shot glasses and she looked pale beneath her tan, but she nodded and stood. "I'm okay."

"Where are you going?"

"I'm going to see if I can help." She blinked as if she was having trouble waking from a nightmare. Then she shook her head.

Adele hurried across the destroyed terrace to the man who'd been shot.

I reached for Consuela, held her close, and felt her enormous little heart beating against my chest. "I need to help too."

"*Yip.*" She understood.

I put her down on a chair that was miraculously unscathed and followed Adele.

My friend knelt in a pool of blood, applying pressure to a wound.

"What do you need?"

"Clean linen."

None of the linen on the terrace qualified.

"I'll look inside."

The lobby was a long hallway ending in an ornate staircase and a marble-topped check-in counter. It seemed oddly familiar. There was not a soul in sight.

I took another step. Glass crunched beneath the soles of my shoes. "Hello," I called.

No one answered.

A trail of blood led down the hallway. I certainly didn't want to go that way. Instead, I peeked into a bright airy room.

There were tables set for dinner; I snatched tablecloths and napkins. The silverware clattered to the floor.

I pushed through the survivors on the veranda. Some were crying. Others cradled injured limbs.

One man wasn't moving, his eyes stared sightlessly at the porch's painted ceiling.

I draped one of the tablecloths over his body.

Nearby, a woman was digging through the wreckage of her table with her right hand. "I can't find my phone. I can't find my phone. I can't find my phone." She held a phone in her left.

The sirens were close, but not close enough.

I sank onto the concrete next to Adele.

"Thanks." She took the linens without looking up from her patient. "When the police or EMTs get here, he needs help right away. Can you tell them?"

"Got it." I picked up Consuela and stumbled out onto the lawn.

When the first police car arrived, I rushed up to the officer who opened the passenger door—Officer Becker, according to the gold nametag on his chest. "There's a man on the front porch who's been shot. I think it's pretty bad."

His gaze traveled from me, a young woman clutching a Chihuahua and an Hermès bag, to the destroyed G-Wagon to the destroyed terrace. "I'll call it in."

"My friend's an emergency room nurse," I continued. "She said the man needed help right away."

Officer Becker spoke into the radio attached to his shoulder, requesting additional units, ambulances, and—he glanced at the G-Wagon—a homicide unit. When he was done, he looked at me. "What happened?"

I pointed to the G-Wagon, told him about the Range Rover, the men, and the guns. I talked until I spotted an EMT climbing out of a just-arrived ambulance. "I need to take him to Adele." I left Officer Becker before he had a chance to respond.

On the veranda, the EMT pushed through the crowd of still-stunned people and knelt next to Adele.

A moment later, Adele stood. Her dress was soaked in

blood and her hands were crimson. Her eyes were still too big for her face. She stumbled toward me. "I did my best."

"Is he—"

"I don't think he's going to make it."

I pulled her out of the way as additional emergency personnel pushed a gurney onto the terrace.

"Let's give our statements and get you home." News vans were arriving. Adele didn't need to be on television. Not covered in blood. Not the week before her wedding.

I found Officer Becker on the veranda and tapped him on the shoulder. "Excuse me."

"Yeah."

"I'm taking my friend home."

He eyed Adele's blood-soaked dress and frowned. "Are either of you hurt?"

"No."

His frown deepened. "Sorry, I can't let you go."

I understood. I did. But I also understood the press would have a field day if I was photographed in the midst of this. Then there was the not-inconsequential concern of Adele moving from the society page to the front page. Her momma would not approve.

"Where's the detective in charge?"

He pointed to a man peering into the G-Wagon.

Across St. Charles, a news van parked at the curb.

"Can she at least go inside?"

Again, he frowned. "Crime scene."

"Adele—" I led her to a chair "—sit here and don't move. I'll be right back."

She nodded and folded herself onto the chair.

"Here, hold Consuela."

Consuela, her eyes bright, settled into Adele's arms and yipped softly as if she understood her role—to comfort.

I reached into my handbag, pushed my gun aside, and grabbed an enormous pair of sunglasses. When they were perched on my nose, I marched across the lawn and waited for the detective to notice me.

I gave him thirty seconds, then cleared my throat.

He turned and looked at me. He was about thirty and Dennis-Quaid-as-Remy-McSwain handsome, good-looking in an I'm-likely-to-lie-to-you-and-trample-your-heart way. I located the hinge in my jaw and snapped my mouth closed.

"Who are you?" he asked.

I glanced back at Adele and Consuela. Adele had buried her face in Consuela's fur. "I'm Poppy Fields."

The detective frowned. "Yeah, right. What's your real name?" He might look like Remy McSwain, but he was nowhere near as charming. Remy would have smiled at me and said, "Sure you are, *chére*."

"My name is Poppy Fields. I was having a drink with a friend when this—" I waved my hand at the wrecked G-Wagon, the wrecked veranda, the windows reduced to shards of glass "—happened. I'd like to give my statement and leave."

"You'll have to wait your turn."

"Listen," I held out my hands and pretended not see the blood ringing my fingernails, "my friend is a nurse and she was helping the man on the terrace who was shot. She's covered in blood. She's traumatized. And I'd like to take her home."

He stared at me for a moment. "What did you see?"

I told him everything that had happened and included descriptions of the man who'd run from the G-Wagon and the man who'd stood at the doorway to the hotel. When I was done, he rubbed his chin. "Is that it?"

Was that sarcasm I heard in his voice? "Look, I'm in town for a week. I'll give you my cell phone number. Please, I'd like to take Adele home."

His gaze sharpened. "Adele?"

"Adele Coombs. I'm here for her wedding."

"Pete Coombs's daughter?"

"Yes."

"Go. But I'll be in touch. Soon."

"Thank you, Detective—" I paused "—I don't know your name."

"René Langlois."

"Thanks for letting us go, Detective Langlois."

He shrugged off my thanks. "If you're a friend of Pete Coombs's, I reckon you better call me René."

I was really Pete's daughter's friend. "Thank you, René."

I felt his gaze on me as I walked back to Adele. "The detective said we could leave."

"I'm going to the hospital with him." She pointed to the man being wheeled past us.

I looked out at the lawn and St. Charles Avenue. There were police and emergency personnel and reporters everywhere. Especially reporters. They were multiplying like rabbits. "I'll drive you. Can we get out through the back?"

Adele reached into her handbag, pulled out a fob, and held it out to me. "Take the car key. I'm going in the ambulance."

"Adele—"

"I'm going with the ambulance," she repeated.

"But—"

"I can tell the doctors exactly what I did for him." Adele might look like a delicate doll, but her spine was made of forged steel. There was no point in arguing with her when her mind was set.

"Fine." I opened my palm. "I'll follow you."

She dropped the fob into my hand and followed the gurney down the steps, speaking over her shoulder. "Don't do that. There's no telling how long I'll be. Go home. I'll call you later."

I watched her stop and exchange a few words with René Langlois, I watched her convince the EMTs to let her ride in the ambulance, and I watched the vehicle drive away.

"C'mon." I tucked Consuela into my arms and we escaped the chaos on the veranda. Inside, the same eerie sense of having been there before stopped me in my tracks. "This place seems so familiar."

"*Yip.*"

"It's the movie." A uniformed officer stepped into the hallway and regarded me with suspicion.

"The movie?"

"*Pretty Baby* was filmed here."

Chariss had made me sit through every Louis Malle film ever made. Multiple times. I *knew* this house. I'd watched a twelve-year-old Brooke Shields run through this house. I knew the way to the backyard.

Except the police officer blocked my path. "I'll have to ask you to step outside, ma'am."

"Detective Langlois said I could go." He hadn't said I could cut through the hotel, but that was just a detail. A detail not worth mentioning. "I won't touch anything. I promise. You can walk me to the back door." I offered up a tremulous smile.

Consuela regarded him with pleading button eyes.

We were a one-two punch of feminine wiles.

He caved. "This way."

I followed the officer through the hotel and stepped into a backyard blessedly free of reporters. "Thank you."

"You have a car nearby?"

"It's parked on the street."

He nodded and scanned the charming backyard for gun-toting killers. Finding none, he said, "Take care, ma'am."

A gate led to the sidewalk (which Adele insisted on calling a banquette).

Two minutes later, I was behind the wheel of Adele's Cayenne with Consuela perched in the passenger seat next to me. I fastened my seatbelt and leaned my head back against the soft leather.

"*Grrr.*"

"What's wrong?" I asked.

Consuela turned her head and looked into the backseat.

I glanced in the rearview mirror.

A man—the man who'd crawled out of the G-Wagon—rose up from the floorboards and pressed his gun against my head.

The metal on my skin was cool in the stuffy car. I shivered. "What do you want?" I held up my shaking hands.

"Start the car."

I met his dark gaze in the mirror. "I'll give you the keys. Take the car. Just let us go."

The man snorted his opinion of that idea. "Start the car."

With a trembling finger, I pushed the ignition button and the Porsche purred to life.

"Drive."

I tightened my clammy hands around the wheel. "Where?"

"The docks."

My gaze shifted to my handbag on the seat next to Consuela. So close, but much too far. "I don't know where that is."

"Take Tchoupitoulas."

"Take what?"

The pressure of the gun against my temple increased. "Drive toward the river."

That I understood. I pulled onto the street. "There's a roadblock ahead." The police had closed access to St. Charles.

"Turn around."

"This is a one-way street."

"Do it," he growled.

He had the gun. I pulled into a driveway and turned the car the wrong direction.

"Take a right on Carondelet."

I did as I was told.

"Now take a right on Foucher."

We headed back toward St. Charles, but a police car, white with bright blue lettering, blocked access to the avenue. When traffic cleared, we'd be able to cross or turn left. "What do I do?"

"Cross."

He leaned back, presumably so the patrolman who directed traffic wouldn't see the gun pointed at my head.

I glanced at Consuela.

She stared back at me, then hopped from her seat to the floorboards.

I took a breath. It was now or never. I jammed my foot onto the gas pedal and the car shot forward. A quick jerk of the wheel and Adele's new Porsche, a wedding gift from her fiancé, slammed into the parked police car.

Bang! The air in the car reverberated with the gun's shot.

The deploying airbag knocked me backward and emptied my lungs.

For a few long seconds, I gasped for air. Then I groped for my handbag.

"Bitch!"

The Porsche's back door opened.

My fingers closed around my gun.

Bang!

The man was out of the car and he was shooting, but not at me. The damned airbag—I couldn't see what was happening.

Bang!

Somehow, I unfastened my seatbelt, opened the door, and stumbled onto the pavement.

The man who'd been in my backseat strode toward the fallen patrol officer. The officer clutched his side with one hand and barely hung on to his gun with the other.

There was no doubt in my mind what happened next. "Stop!"

My unwanted passenger stopped. He turned at my voice. He pointed his gun at me.

My breath caught in my throat, adrenaline roared through my system, the sounds around me faded to quiet.

He lifted his gun another inch.

I shot him.

Chapter Two

I spent the first fourteen years of my life in Montana. With my dad. I loved pleasing my father, and I learned quickly what pleased him most was my winning shooting competitions. I also learned, with practice, I could shoot better than just about anyone.

The decade since Dad's death hadn't affected my aim.

The man who'd shot the police officer jerked backward and fell to the pavement.

My stomach fell with him.

Everything my dad ever taught me, everything I knew about guns, everything I knew about bad guys, went into that shot. What I'd learned from my dad: if you're going to point a gun at another human being, be sure you mean it. What I'd learned from working for Mr. Brown: shoot to kill.

Knowing and feeling were two different things. I'd killed someone, and I felt sick—wobbly, regretting-that-Pimm's-cup sick.

The wounded police officer simply gaped at me. Maybe

that was all he could do. The hand pressed against his side was stained a wet crimson and he was shaking.

"Put the gun down!"

Two new police officers had guns aimed at me.

My stomach lurched again. This was supposed to be a last-hurrah trip before I went into Mr. Brown's version of spy boot camp. I was supposed to drink cocktails, eat ridiculous amounts of decadent food, and flirt with handsome southern men named Beau or Luke or Atticus.

Instead, I'd shot a man dead and two uniformed police officers looked as if they might shoot me.

Not that I blamed them. They'd just arrived and hadn't seen who shot their fellow officer. All they saw was a wounded comrade, a man with a hole between his eyes, and a woman with a gun.

"I'm putting it down." I bent slowly and placed my gun on the pavement, carefully so as not to scratch the mother-of-pearl handle. Then I stepped back.

"Hands up!" barked one of the officers. He had a mustache positively quivering with outrage.

I raised my hands above my head.

"Kick the gun toward me." Mustache was very bossy, and very crazy if he thought I was kicking a pearl-handled gun across the rough pavement.

"She saved me," said the bleeding officer.

"She what?" Mustache's disbelieving tone was a bit offensive.

"She took him out with one shot." The injured man nodded toward the dead one.

"How bad are you hurt?" asked Mustache.

"A bullet grazed my ribs."

Well, that was a relief. "May I lower my hands?"

"Don't move."

The scents of car exhaust and testosterone swirled around me. I didn't move a muscle.

Mustache stepped forward and picked up my gun. The other newly arrived officer, one who was too young to possess such ancient blue eyes, stared at me as if he'd never seen a woman in a DVF jumpsuit before. Granted, I'd ignored Adele's southern dress memo—the one requiring women to wear bright colors, ruffles, floral prints, or lots of monograms—but my jumpsuit wasn't daring (*that* daring) or revealing.

"I saw you on television," said Old Blue Eyes.

"That was probably my mother."

He shook his head. "You're Poppy Fields."

He had seen me on TV. "Yes. May I lower my hands now?"

He nodded. "Fine."

"Wait!" Mustache glared at his partner. "Who is she?"

"That party girl who got abducted by the Sinaloan drug lord."

What a description.

Mustache narrowed his eyes and reassessed my threat factor. The Louboutin heels, the DVF jumpsuit, the Hermès bag swinging from the crook of my arm, the wrecked Cayenne.

He lowered his gun. "Fine. Put your hands down."

I lowered my hands slowly and glanced at the wrecked SUV. "May I get my dog? Please? I want to make sure she's okay."

"Your dog?"

"Consuela. She's still in the car." Had she been hurt when I crashed the Porsche?

"I'll get her," said Mustache.

"I wouldn't." My voice held a warning.

"Why not?"

"She doesn't like mustaches." I took a step toward the car.

He held up a hand, stopping me. "What kind of dog?"

"A Chihuahua."

The man snorted into his mustache, brushed past me, and reached into the car.

Consuela launched herself out of the wrecked Porsche, a whirl of fluffy caramel fur, sharp teeth, and snarls.

Mustache stumbled backward—and backward.

Somehow, Consuela had attached herself to his chest.

His arms pinwheeled—and pinwheeled.

Thunk! He fell onto the trying-to-be-grassy strip by the streetcar track (Adele insisted on calling the area neutral ground).

Taking Mustache down wasn't enough for my killer Chihuahua. Her teeth were bared. Her fur stood straight up. She was in full attack mode.

"Consuela! No!"

Consuela suffered from situational deafness. Right now, she was definitely deaf. Or maybe she couldn't hear me above her own growls. More likely she chose not to. She opened her little jaws and lunged for Mustache's face.

He warded her off with his forearm.

My dog sunk her teeth through the powder blue material of Mustache's shirt and into the fleshy part of his arm.

"Son of a bitch!"

The other officer's eyes were enormous—big as saucers. He approached Mustache with his gun still drawn.

Surely he wouldn't shoot my dog! "Consuela! Stop it! No!"

Consuela shook her head from side to side.

Mustache shook his arm up and down.

"Consuela!" I dashed toward them, caught my heel in a crack in the pavement, and barely stopped myself from falling. Pain shot through my ankle. I was getting over a bad sprain and had been told—definitively—not to wear high heels. A directive I'd ignored for this trip. I hopped on my good leg. "Consuela!"

She ignored me.

Mustache let loose a string of expletives that would make a longshoreman blush.

"*Grrr.*" Consuela's vocabulary might be limited, but she gave as good as she got.

"What the hell is going on?"

Old Blue Eyes turned and lowered his gun. Immediately.

Mustache stopped shaking his arm.

I stumbled forward and scooped my dog off Mustache's chest.

Detective René Langlois' face was flushed. His brows were drawn. He looked angry. And not mildly miffed angry. More like pissed-as-hell angry. "I asked a question."

Three police officers answered as one. Too bad none of them were saying the same thing.

I held Consuela out in front of me until our gazes were level. "Bad dog."

"*Yip.*" She was unrepentant.

I narrowed my eyes. "Bad dog."

"*Yip.*" She'd do it again in a heartbeat.

"Miss Fields."

I tore my gaze away from Consuela's I-could-have-taken-him glare and looked at Detective Langlois. "Yes?"

"What happened?"

"He—" I cradled Consuela with one arm and pointed at the man I'd shot with the other "—was hiding in my car. He put a gun to my head and told me to take him to the docks. But I ran into the police car instead." Now I pointed at the unfortunate juncture of crumpled metal. "He got out and wounded—I'm sorry, I don't know your name."

"Officer Wells," supplied the bloodied police officer.

"He shot Officer Wells. I told him to stop. He pointed the gun at me. And I shot him."

"Where did you get a gun?"

"My handbag." My Hermès bag still hung from the crook of my arm.

Detective Langlois pinched the bridge of his nose. "And the dog?"

"Consuela."

"She attacked a police officer."

"I did warn him. She doesn't like mustaches."

"*Grrr.*"

"She's right. I heard her—" A quelling scowl from Detective Langlois silenced the officer with blue eyes.

"Do you have a permit for that gun, Miss Fields?"

"I do."

"In what state?"

"California."

Detective Langlois rubbed the heel of his palm across his eyes. "So, if I've got this straight, since I saw you fifteen minutes ago, you've been abducted, shot a man dead with an illegal firearm, and your dog attacked a police officer."

He'd left out wrecking the Porsche and a police cruiser, but I wasn't about to quibble. "My gun isn't illegal."

"It is in the state of Louisiana."

Uh-oh.

"She saved my life," said Officer Wells.

Saving a police officer had to count for something.

Detective Langlois (calling him by his first name didn't seem wise right now) snorted, then looked down at the dead man. "Where did you learn to shoot?"

"My father taught me."

"Your father taught you to shoot people right between the eyes?"

"My father taught me that if I point a gun at a person, I'd better mean it."

Detective Langlois scowled at the body. "Vic Klein knows you meant it."

Officer Wells' sharp inhalation of breath had us all looking at him. "That's Vic Klein?"

The detective shifted his scowl my way. "That's Vic Klein."

I swallowed. "Who?"

His eyes searched my face. "You don't know who he is?"

"No idea."

"He's a heroin smuggler and dealer. We've been trying to pin something on him since he arrived here."

"Oh."

"You don't seem all that upset." Detective Langlois's eyes narrowed. "Most people—they kill someone—they're upset."

The deep creases at the corners of Detective Langlois's eyes worried me—that and the tight edges of his lips. Did he think I was some sort of sociopathic party girl who shot people for thrills?

I shifted my gaze away from the man I'd killed. The live oaks planted in the neutral ground cast thin shadows. A forgotten strand of Mardi Gras beads tangled among the leaves of the tallest tree. Behind me, a red-brick church surrounded by a wrought-iron fence took up an enormous lot. Directly across the street, Spanish-looking houses hid behind crepe myrtles. And, to our right, Detective Langlois's first crime scene occupied the press—for now. How long would that last? "Of course I'm upset."

Detective Langlois's left eyebrow rose.

I snuggled Consuela close to my chest. "Officer Wells will tell you I shot in self-defense."

Officer Wells nodded. "She saved my life."

"We're going to have to take you in."

The problem with working for a secret government agency was that it was secret. I couldn't just whisper NSA or CIA or

FBI in Detective Langlois's ear. I couldn't tell him about my boss, Mr. Brown. I was supposed to be a party girl, the kind of woman no one took seriously. It was the ultimate cover.

If I blew that cover when I wasn't even on assignment, my usefulness would be at an end and Mr. Brown's head might explode.

All of which meant a trip to the police station was in my future. "Okay. Fine. I need to sit down anyway." I swayed on my feet as if I might collapse any second.

The blue-eyed officer hurried toward me, his arms outstretched.

Mustache moved toward me too, but Consuela's growl stopped him dead in his tracks.

Detective Langlois's lips twitched.

"Do you think we'll be done by eight? I'm supposed to meet Adele and her parents for dinner." The plan had been drinks at the Columns and dinner at Antoine's. Adele being covered in blood and riding to the hospital in an ambulance had probably changed that plan. But it didn't hurt to mention Pete Coombs—not when his name had been my ticket away from the Columns.

"You're gonna be late."

Which was just as well. I wasn't exactly looking forward to telling Adele I'd wrecked her new Cayenne. On purpose.

"How late? I should probably text them."

"A man is dead." Detective Langlois kept reminding me of that—as if I could forget with the corpse in front of me. "You killed him."

I knew that. My stomach was tied in knots over that. "Would it make you feel better if I was hysterical?"

Again, his lips twitched. "It might."

I knew exactly what Detective Langlois saw standing in front of him—a spoiled young woman draped in expensive clothing with a ten-thousand-dollar handbag swinging from the crook of one arm and a more-spoiled-than-she-was dog tucked into the crook of the other. He saw a woman more concerned with her dinner reservation than the end of a man's life.

If I were an actress like my mother, now would be the time I'd manufacture some tears. Instead I cuddled Consuela closer. "Just because you can't see my emotions doesn't mean I don't have them."

Detective Langlois stared at me for endless seconds. "Officer Samuels!"

Mustache jumped to attention. "Yes, sir?"

"Take Wells to the hospital." Detective Langlois's gaze landed on Consuela. "I assume that animal is current on its shots?"

"*Grrr*."

"Shhh," I told her. "She is."

He nodded and returned his gaze to Mustache—Officer Samuels. "While you're there, get that bite treated." He swung his gaze to Wells. "Quickly, tell me exactly what happened."

"I was waving traffic off St. Charles—"

"Quickly, Officer Wells. The SparkNotes version."

"The Porsche slammed into the cruiser. That guy—" Officer Wells pointed at Vic Klein's body "—exited the vehicle's backseat and shot at me. I think he nicked a rib. Then she—" he smiled in my direction "—got out of the Porsche and told him to stop. He pointed his gun at her. She shot him."

"Thank you, Wells."

"It was a clear case of self-defense."

"Thank you, Wells."

"If she hadn't interfered, I might be dead."

"Thank you, Wells."

"But—"

"Go to the hospital, Wells." He turned to me. "Where are you staying, Miss Fields?"

"A house on Royal Street."

He waited.

"I don't know the address." Ditsy party girl? Mission accomplished.

"You don't know where you're staying?"

"I'd know the house if I saw it."

"Are you renting it?"

"Not exactly. I'm borrowing it."

"Someone lent you their house?"

"James Ballester." James and my mother had made four movies together. Each one had grossed more than five hundred million dollars. After Hurricane Katrina, when rebuilding New Orleans earned Hollywood merit badges, James had bought the house on Royal. It was enormous, and old, and he assured me it was haunted. A housekeeper, improbably named Ladybug, and a cook, Chester, lived there full-time. James visited a couple of weekends each year.

"Do movie stars regularly loan you houses, Miss Fields?"

Honesty seemed the best policy. "Yes."

"She's Poppy Fields."

"I know her name, Officer Matthews."

"She's Chariss Carlton's daughter. She's the one who got abducted by the Sinaloan drug lord."

Detective Langlois's eyes narrowed. A dead drug dealer lay at his feet—one who'd imported heroin. Probably from Sinaloa. Did he think I was on some sort of vigilante quest to bring down the Sinaloa Cartel?

"I'm here for Adele's wedding. That's it."

Detective Langlois rubbed his chin. "It's Thursday, Miss Fields."

I assumed that was a rhetorical observation and said nothing.

"Usually Thursdays are slow." He shook his head. "But this Thursday, I've got three bodies. Maybe four."

"Four?"

"I got the guy behind the wheel of the Mercedes G-Wagon, Vic—" he pointed in case I'd forgotten I'd just killed a man "—the dead man on the porch, and possibly the man Adele Coombs accompanied to the hospital."

"Oh."

"According to the people at the Columns, I've also got a crazed army running amok in the Garden District."

Amok? "Not an army. Just six."

"Says you." He rubbed his chin again. "About you..."

"What about me?"

"You were the only person on that porch who could give me a clear-eyed description of what happened."

I assumed his was a rhetorical observation and said nothing.

"Makes me wonder. How is it a Hollywood party girl keeps her cool during an attack like that?"

Not rhetorical, but I had no answer. I stared mutely.

"How is it that same party girl takes out a criminal not fifteen minutes later?"

I tightened my hold on Consuela.

"You got any ideas on that, Miss Fields?"

This conversation was going nowhere good. "I'm observant and unlucky."

His eyes narrowed. "You can go, but—"

"Let me guess. I can't leave town?"

"You read my mind, Miss Fields."

I nodded. Once.

"I'll have someone take you home."

"Thank you, Detective Langlois. I don't suppose I can have my gun back."

"No, Miss Fields. I don't suppose you can."

"*Miss Fields! Poppy Fields!*"

My knotted stomach sank to my ankles. The reporters and their cameramen had found me. I adjusted my sunglasses. It was too little, too late. I'd be on the late local news. Then I'd be on *TMZ*.

"*Poppy! What are you doing in New Orleans?*"

I glared at Detective Langlois (the effect lost behind the dark lenses of my Gold and Wood glasses), gritted my teeth, and spoke without moving my lips. "May I leave now? Please?"

"*Poppy! Did you witness a crime?*"

"Please? May I go?"

The cameras shifted their angles from me to Vic Klein's body and back again.

Detective Langlois had said Klein imported heroin. Javier Diaz, the current head of the Sinaloan Carter, a man who already wanted me dead, was sure to see the pictures. If Klein worked for him, Diaz might redouble his efforts.

"Please?" Desperation colored my voice.

"Fine." Detective Langlois glanced back at the horde of reporters. "I'll take you home."

"Don't you have crime scenes to work?"

"Would you prefer to climb into the back of a cruiser?"

In front of the reporters? That would be a disaster. "Thank you for the offer, Detective. Can we leave? Now? Please?"

"*Poppy! Did you kill someone?*"

A truthful answer would land me on the front page of *USA TODAY* and every tabloid in the supermarket.

Chapter Three

James had hired a New Orleans design firm to decorate his ten-room house on Royal Street. The result was impressive. Soft beige walls rose to impossibly high ceilings. Chandeliers dripped crystals. Floor-to-ceiling windows welcomed light and air and led to wrought-iron balconies exploding with flowers. French antiques covered in improbable fabrics shared floor space with more modern pieces. The art was local, bright, and very good.

I closed James's front door on Detective Langlois, put Consuela down, and dug through my handbag for my phone.

The calls I had to make would be easier with a glass of wine —a bottle of wine. But that would be cowardly and irresponsible and weak.

I straightened my shoulders, pressed the correct button on the phone's screen, and listened to the sound of ringing.

"Brown." He answered on the first ring.

I didn't have time to figure out what I was going to say. "It's Poppy," I squeaked. "Poppy Fields."

"What's wrong, Miss Fields?" Was that resignation I heard

in his voice? Mr. Brown had recruited me into his super-secret agency. He'd wanted a girl who'd fit seamlessly into the lives of the ultra-rich (and sometimes crooked). A girl no one would suspect of spying. I was the answer. Sometimes, I sensed he regretted his decision. Like now.

I swallowed. "I shot someone."

Seconds ticked by. "Who?"

"A man named Vic Klein. He was about to murder a police officer."

"I see."

He didn't see. Not at all. "The police tell me Vic Klein smuggled heroin."

Mr. Brown's answering silence was deafening.

"It's possible—" I swallowed again "—I'll be on the evening news."

Mr. Brown sighed. A long-suffering sigh. All things considered, I preferred his silence.

"There were reporters," I explained.

"What do you need?"

"Nothing. I don't need anything. I just thought you should know." I walked toward the wine fridge.

"I see. Is that all?"

There was a chilled bottle of sauvignon blanc calling my name—*Poppy, Poppy*. "Yes."

"Were you arrested?"

I poured the wine into a glass. All the way to the rim. "No. I told you, Klein was about to kill a policeman."

The sound of tapping keys carried through the phone line. That was the only sound.

I sipped.

"Vic Klein?"

"Yes."

"I'm sending Stone." Mark Stone and I had worked

together in Paris. He was brave and smart and looked exactly like Chris Hemsworth.

"What? No! I'm here for a wedding. I can't just throw a plus-one at Adele and her family." Especially now.

"Yes, you can." Mr. Brown didn't sound as if arguing was an option.

Thor. Here. That called for another large sip of wine.

"Diaz already wanted you dead," Mr. Brown continued. "And you just shot one of his top lieutenants."

"You're sure Vic Klein worked for the Sinaloans?"

"He ran their Chicago operation till about two years ago when he moved to New Orleans."

"Why would the Sinaloans import through New Orleans?" It was a valid question. Sinaloa was on the western side of Mexico. It wasn't as if they could cast off and sail across the Gulf. They had to sail around Mexico and through the Panama Canal before they even reached the Gulf. "Are you sure he wasn't working for someone else?"

Who are you to question our intel? The unspoken question was extremely loud.

"I thought the Sinaloans imported over land through El Paso and Nogales. Why would they start shipping product?"

"Maybe they're diversifying their transportation." Mr. Brown's tone said the discussion was over.

I'd read somewhere about a Mexican drug lord with his own fleet of submarines. That seemed sneaky. Loading heroin onto a cargo ship seemed fraught with pitfalls—the ship could sink, the load could fail inspection at the port, the cargo could be confiscated. Meanwhile, bales of heroin marked with beacons could be tossed out of a cargo plane at little or no risk to the pilot. And, with multiple drop points, there was little chance of losing a whole load. "You'd think if they were diversifying, they'd do it with airplanes, not ships."

"Miss Fields—"

"Yes, Mr. Brown."

"Stone will arrive tomorrow. Where are you staying?"

I really ought to learn the address. "At James Ballester's house in the French Quarter."

I heard more tapping as Mr. Brown looked up James's address.

"Expect him by tomorrow afternoon."

I said nothing. I was not happy.

"And Miss Fields?"

"Yes, Mr. Brown."

"Try not to shoot anyone else." He hung up the phone before I could think of a snappy reply.

One call down. One to go.

I dialed Chariss's number.

The phone rang and rang. Did she not have voicemail enabled?

I composed a text in my head—Chariss, I shot someone today and I may make the news. I'm fine. Don't worry. Say hi to Yurgi for me. xoxo. Chariss's billionaire Russian boyfriend was actually a nice man. I liked him far more than any of the other men Chariss had welcomed into her life over the years. He was smart and funny and he adored her.

"Hello." Chariss's voice was muffled.

"It's Poppy."

"Do you have any idea what time it is?"

"No. Where are you?"

"We're on Yurgi's yacht." Which was a high-handed way of saying she didn't know what time it was either. "Why are you calling?"

"I ran into a bit of trouble today."

"I thought you were in New Orleans for your friend's wedding."

"I am."

"What trouble could you get into there?"

"I shot someone."

"You what?" The question was shrill, and it was easy to picture her stalking the deck and scowling at the stars.

"He was a bad guy. I saved a policeman."

"And?"

"There were reporters. I wanted to let you know before you saw something on the news or read about it online."

Her silence was even more disapproving than Mr. Brown's.

"I'm not hurt." She hadn't asked, but I told her anyway.

"Do you need a lawyer?"

"No. There won't be any charges filed." I crossed my fingers.

"Why do these things keep happening to you, Poppy?" Chariss actually sounded worried.

"Wrong place, wrong time." Chariss knowing about Vic Klein's possible ties to a man who wanted me dead would only cause her worry. "I'm fine."

"Sure you are."

"I am," I insisted. And I was.

"It doesn't bother you? Shooting someone?"

"Of course it bothers me." Maybe not as much as it should—Vic Klein had been a bad man—but it definitely bothered me.

"What do your friend and her family think about this?"

"I haven't told them yet. We're going to dinner tonight."

"Where?"

"Antoine's."

"Charming place. James takes me there when I visit." If Chariss said Antoine's was charming, it was the kind of restaurant where movie stars could dine without being accosted by enthusiastic fans or paparazzi.

A voice—a Russian voice—carried through the line and

Charis giggled. "Listen, dear. I'm going to let you go." Her voice was husky.

The Russian voice said something else.

Chariss giggled. Again. Chariss never giggled. "Yurgi, stop."

I didn't need to hear anything more. "I'll talk to you later. Bye."

I drained half the glass of wine in one sip.

Then I called Adele. Her phone went straight to voicemail. "Hey, it's me. If I don't hear from you, I'll plan on seeing you at Antoine's. Hope everything is okay."

I dropped the phone on the couch and went looking for Ladybug.

I found her in the kitchen with Chester. "Sorry to interrupt." The two were watching *Wheel of Fortune.*

"You're not interrupting." Ladybug rose from her stool. "What can I do for you?"

"A couple of things. A friend is going to be joining me. He'll need his own room."

Ladybug nodded.

"And I'm going to dinner at Antoine's this evening—"

Chester sighed. "I sure would love to cook for you, Miss Fields."

"I'd like that, too. It seems as if Adele has me booked for every meal." I held my hands to Ladybug, part of my plea for help. "About Antoine's—what should I wear?"

She eyed my jumpsuit with obvious disapproval. "Did you bring any dresses?"

"Yes." Half a closet's worth. Traveling light wasn't in my nature. "But I'm not sure—" I knew how to dress for Los Angeles or Paris or London. My jumpsuit, which would have garnered envious stares in any of those cities, had been wrong. And I didn't want to wear the wrong thing tonight—not when I had to tell Adele and her family I'd shot a man—killed a man. Unless I'd made the news. If I made the news, they already knew. If I made the news, the paparazzi would descend. If I made the news, I wouldn't blame the Coombs if they canceled dinner and sent me packing. And if that didn't do it, there was the Porsche with less than five hundred miles on the odometer that I'd crumpled.

"I'd be happy to take a look." Ladybug's voice brought me back to the here and now.

"Thank you."

She followed me to my closet and eyed the choices.

"What about that?" I pointed to a strapless sequined tea-length dress designed by Naeem Khan.

"Too dressy."

She reached into the closest and pulled out a lavender metallic tweed Lela Rose dress. I'd bought it on a whim, brought it on a whim. "This is the one. You have pearls?"

The dress wasn't one I would have selected. I was definitely in the weeds. I took the dress from her. "What about lunch tomorrow?"

"Where are you going?"

"Galatoire's?"

She huffed. "Friday lunch at Galatoire's? You waiting in line?"

"Waiting in line?"

"Galatoire's doesn't take reservations. Who's taking you?"

"The Coombs."

She nodded. "They'll be paying someone to wait for them."

"Paying someone to wait? In line?"

"Going rate is ten dollars a head plus tip." Her gaze returned to the closet. She skipped right over the Jason Wu mini-dress I'd planned on wearing. Instead she pulled out a floral cotton Oscar de la Renta. "For tomorrow, this one will have to do."

She scanned the remaining dresses and tsked.

"I brought the wrong things."

She chuckled. "There's a Saks on Canal Street."

"I'll go tomorrow."

She nodded her approval. "Ask for Lillian."

At five minutes till eight, I presented myself to the maître d' at Antoine's. "I'm part of the Coombs party."

He glanced down at his book and his brows rose. "You've been moved from the Rex Room to the Tabasco Room."

I didn't know what that meant, but I followed a tuxedoed waiter through the main dining room, down a hallway, and into a small red—Tabasco red—room with black woodwork and gilt chandeliers.

The room held a table set for two.

"I think there's been some mistake. I'm dining with the Coombs family."

"No mistake, miss."

"With whom am I dining?" Was Adele going to gently tell me my bridesmaid services were no longer needed? Not that I blamed her. The photographers grappling for a picture of me would turn her wedding into a circus.

"I'm not sure, miss."

"She's dining with me."

The waiter and I turned and looked at the entrance.

The man who'd spoken strode into the room and took my hand. "I'm Carter's cousin, Knox Arnaut." The man who'd claimed my hand wore a crisp white shirt, a navy blazer, khakis, and a smile that could melt hearts.

"Knox? Like the fort?"

He grinned, showing off impossibly white teeth. "Now, I know a woman named Poppy Fields is not making fun of my name."

"Of course not. It's a pleasure to meet you." I glanced at the table. "Where is everyone?"

Knox looked at the waiter. "May we please have two Sazeracs, Charles?"

"Yes, sir." The waiter left us.

"Adele's mother took to her bed. Adele is still at the hospital. Carter is with her. Mr. Coombs is still barking at the police commissioner. Without the four of them, it was hardly a family dinner."

"Why didn't someone just call and cancel?"

"Somewhere between the Columns and the hospital, Adele lost her cell." Knox shrugged his broad shoulders. "I'm afraid she doesn't have your number memorized, so no one could call you about the change in plans."

I didn't believe him. Adele was probably working up the nerve to fire me. "It was nice of you to come, but if you've got something you'd rather be—"

"There is nothing I'd rather do tonight than have dinner with you. Have you been to Antoine's before?"

"No. This is my first trip to New Orleans."

"Well, hopefully the rest of your stay will be more pleasant." Knox pulled out one of the chairs and looked at me expectantly.

I sank into the waiting chair and murmured, "Thank you."

He joined me at the table. "Antoine's is one of the oldest family-run restaurants in the United States. It dates back to 1840. And—" he leaned forward as if he were about to share a secret "—it's haunted."

"Really?"

Something in my tone must have said *yeah, right* because Knox's eyes widened. "Now, don't go telling me you don't believe in ghosts."

"Fine, I won't tell you."

He wagged a callused finger at me. "Now, now, not a wise thing to be a disbeliever in New Orleans. The ghosts might decide to show you they're real."

"If they do, I'll change my mind."

The waiter appeared with our drinks.

When he'd presented us with menus and departed, Knox raised his glass. "To Adele's beautiful friend."

"To Carter's handsome cousin."

We touched the rims of our glasses and I sipped. "What's in this drink?"

"Sazerac rye, a cube of sugar, absinthe, Peychaud's Bitters, and lemon peel."

"Absinthe?"

"Just a touch." He measured a tiny amount between two fingers.

"What do you do, Knox?"

"I'm a lawyer."

I blinked back my surprise. Given his deep tan, I would have guessed he spent his days hunting or playing golf. "A lawyer?"

"You don't like lawyers?"

"I don't know many." And the ones I knew were mostly entertainment lawyers, by all accounts a breed apart. "What kind of law do you practice?"

"I'm with the district attorney's office."

I took another sip of Sazerac.

"You have that look."

"What look?"

"The look that says you think I'm the next Huey Long."

I wiped all expression from my face. "Who's Huey Long?"

"Seriously?"

I nodded.

"You never saw or read *All the King's Men*?"

"Nope." It was just a small lie.

Knox puffed his chest. "Huey Long was a somewhat corrupt politician here in Louisiana."

Somewhat? "Really?"

"He was assassinated."

"You don't say?"

"His son Russell held his father's Senate seat for forty years."

That I hadn't known. I widened my eyes.

"And you know all this."

I smiled. "Guilty."

"For that I'm taking you to Muriel's after dinner."

"Muriel's?"

"For an after-dinner drink in the séance lounge."

I made no comment.

"I'll introduce you to a ghost. Now—" Knox leaned back in his chair "—tell me about what happened today."

"You heard? Everything?" I clenched my hands in my lap. "Was it on the news?"

"Pete Coombs would never allow that." He grinned. "I heard about it around the office. First, I heard my cousin's fiancée was at the Columns during the shooting. What happened?"

I told him.

"How frightening. Did you see anyone? Would you recognize them again?"

"Just Vic Klein."

"The man you shot."

I glanced at my hands in my lap. My knuckles were white. "You heard that too."

"Forgive my saying, but you don't look like the kind of girl who shoots people then goes out to dinner."

I lifted my gaze. "What does that kind of girl look like?"

"Tougher."

"I'm tough."

He smiled at me over the rim of his glass. "Now, don't get riled. You're just too pretty to look tough."

A compliment or an insult? Maybe both? "The police detective told me Klein was a smuggler."

"He was."

"Moving product through the Port of New Orleans?"

Knox winced."Drugs are imported through every port in America. Even ours." He sipped his drink. "There are people who'll look the other way for certain shipments if the price is right."

"How many people would have to be bribed?"

"Lots."

"And how much would that cost?"

"Lots."

"Seems as if there must be easier ways."

"Maybe." He shrugged. "You can fit a lot of drugs in a shipping container."

I shuddered.

"Are you ready to order, Mr. Arnaut?" The waiter held a small notepad and wore an attentive expression.

"May I order for you, Poppy?" He didn't wait for my answer. "We'll start with Oysters Rockefeller, Charles." Knox looked over the menu. "And some souffléed potatoes. Pompano Ponchartrain for Miss Fields and I'll have the lamb chops."

"Will that be all, sir?"

Knox shifted his gaze to me. "Baked Alaska for dessert?"

"No, thank you."

"You're sure? It was invented here. It's very good."

"Well, then."

"And Baked Alaska."

"Very good, sir."

"Thank you, Charles."

The waiter retreated.

"He never told you his name."

Knox blinked rapidly. "Who?"

"The waiter. He never mentioned his name."

"Charles? Charles is always my waiter. His father was my grandfather's waiter. That's how it works here."

I stared at the deep red walls covered in memorabilia and old portraits in gilded frames. This restaurant was older than the states where I'd grown up. There existed here traditions I'd never imagined. "Is Charles also the Coombs's waiter?"

Knox barked a laugh. "No. And if you're smart, you won't mention that near any of the interested parties."

"Why not?"

"The Coombs are on their third generation of Sterlings."

"Sterlings?"

"Both the name and the job pass down. Adele is not inclined to switch to Charles. It has caused some—" his eyes crinkled "—friction."

He wasn't serious.

I searched his face. His eyes had stopped their twinkling.

He was serious. He crossed his heart. "That shooting you were involved in today? It's nothing compared to who will serve Adele and Carter their first meal as man and wife."

I had a horrible stomach-turning sense that he was very wrong—that the shooting was something that might spiral out of control—but I said nothing.

Chapter Four

"Muriel's is only about three blocks away." Knox looked at my shoes, doubt writ clearly on his face.

My shoes, simple Christian Louboutin pumps in nude, weren't impossibly high. Nor were they made for walking. "I'll be fine."

"You're sure?"

"Positive."

He tucked my hand into the crook of his arm and we turned left on Royal Street. "You'll love Muriel's. Maybe the resident ghost will pay us a visit."

"The resident ghost?" I stopped and peered through a shop window. A mannequin wore a floor-length silk robe designed with Gloria Swanson in mind—fitted satin waist, long billowy sleeves. Chariss would love it.

The light from the window illuminated Knox's wry smile. "Still don't believe in ghosts?"

"Seeing is believing." I glanced at the shop's name—The Trashy Diva. I'd have to come back for the robe when the store was open. I allowed Knox to pull me forward.

"The ghost at Muriel's is Pierre Antoine Lepardi Jourdan."

"That seems awfully specific. Why does Pierre haunt a restaurant?"

"The restaurant is in what used to be his house. He lost the place in a card game. His spirit lingers."

I said nothing. Instead I concentrated on not tripping on the flagstones that made up the banquette.

We walked under lacy balconies. Rum and burnt sugar and rot perfumed the air.

"This way." Knox pulled me gently. "We can cut through Pirates Alley."

We stepped into Jackson Square and I stared up at the cathedral. "It looks like the castle at Disney."

"Now, where do you think old Walt got his inspiration? This way." Knox guided me past the fairy-tale cathedral to a building on the far corner of the square. "Prepare to meet a ghost."

Yeah, right.

At the bar (dark, mirrored, and stocked with unusual bottles), Knox ordered me a drink without asking what I wanted. He presented me an orange concoction in a martini glass.

"What is this?"

"The house specialty. It's called a Fleur de Lis."

"What's in it?"

"It's a Champagne cocktail."

I sipped. It was a very sweet Champagne cocktail. After the dessert we'd devoured at Antoine's, I was done with sweet. I smiled—sweetly. "Thank you." I would have much preferred the glass of neat bourbon he'd ordered for himself.

"This way." Knox led me up a flight of stairs to the second floor and into a room bathed in red light. Two gold sarcophagi flanked an elaborate couch upholstered in cherry velvet. Above the couch hung a starburst mirror—one of many. The mirrors reflected leather couches piled with silk cushions, brick walls, and the deep crimson of the curtains. There were velvet poufs and wingback chairs covered in heavy brocade. Lampshades dripped fringe and on the one painted wall (red, of course) an old portrait (gilt frame, of course) held pride of place.

The scents of candle wax and jasmine and age wafted through the still air.

The room was eerie.

The room was positively normal compared to the woman seated in the largest of the wingback chairs.

She wore an ebony lace dress buttoned high at the neck, a profusion of beads, and black lipstick. She regarded me with dark eyes. "You're here." Her husky voice was better suited to a bedroom.

"Do I know you?"

She cackled.

I glanced at Knox. If this was his idea of a joke, it wasn't funny. But Knox's lips were drawn away from his teeth and his eyes were wide. He looked as if he'd unexpectedly encountered something foul. He'd brought me here to meet a ghost not a medium.

The woman snatched at my hand. "Let's see the trouble you brought to the Crescent City."

I opened my mouth—whatever trouble was brewing in New Orleans was none of my doing. I certainly hadn't brought it with me.

"You been here less than a day and you already killed a man."

"How do you know—"

Her chin bobbed, and she tapped her forehead with a bony finger. "I got the sight."

That, or Knox was wrong and Pete Coombs had not been

able to keep the story off the news. My money was on option two. I tugged at my hand.

"What's it gonna hurt, *chére*? Let me take a look." She laughed again and her hair rattled—almost as if she had bones tied in her dark braids.

My hair, especially the hair on my arms, stood on end, but I opened my fingers (and blamed two Sazeracs, a glass of excellent sauvignon blanc, a Champagne cocktail, and Knox Arnaut).

The woman in the chair traced the tip of a talon-like fingernail across my palm. "You're looking, but you don't know what you're looking for."

I rolled my eyes. I couldn't help it. Her pronouncement was exactly the kind of broad, applies-to-everybody banality I'd been expecting. I tugged at my hand.

The woman held tight—death-grip tight.

"You been in a heap of trouble."

Anyone who watched the news, read the paper, or followed social media knew that. My lips thinned.

"More's coming."

Now came the part where she asked for money.

She tapped the center of my palm. "You're fixing to light up this town."

Exactly the opposite of my plan. I intended to quietly attend my friend's wedding then leave. I tugged against her hold. Harder.

The woman's grip on my wrist was an iron shackle. "Ain't nothing you can stop. There's a train loaded with trouble an' it's rolling right at you." She stared into the distance as if she could see the train bearing down on me.

Knox's hand circled my other wrist. "This is ridiculous."

The woman looked up at him and grinned. The light made her teeth look as if they'd been bathed in blood.

Knox flinched. "Let her go."

"Something you don't want her to hear?"

"Of course not. You're scaring her."

Another cackle. "She don't look scared to me."

I wasn't scared. I was...unnerved. The hand circling my wrist was icy; the finger probing my palm was on fire.

The woman looked down at my palm again. "This battle that's coming—" she tapped "—you better win."

"What battle?" And why on earth was I listening to this crap?

"Some would say it's the battle between good and evil."

I gave up tugging and yanked. Yanked hard enough that when the woman unexpectedly let go of my wrist, I took a giant step back. Knox also lost his grip. But he took two giant steps back and landed in a heap on one of the leather couches.

The woman in the chair chuckled and dug in her pocket. "Here—" she held something out to me "—this might keep you safe."

"What is that?" I eyed the little bundle in her palm.

"Good hoodoo."

I glanced back at Knox.

He was smoothing his hair and his jacket, looking for his lost dignity and pretending the woman and I didn't exist.

"Take it," the woman insisted.

I held out my hand. Again, I blamed the liquor, the man, and the eeriness of the encounter. Fill me with coffee and put me in a sunny café and my hand would have stayed shut.

She carefully placed the tiny piece of linen tied with twine in the center of my hand and closed my fingers around it. "Keep it with you."

Again I glanced at Knox. He'd spilled bourbon on his shirt and was regarding the once-white cotton with distaste.

"You ain't leaving this town anytime soon."

Of course I wasn't. As far as I knew, I was still in a wedding.

"I can tell by looking—" the woman lifted her gaze to my face and her eyes found mine "—you don't run from no fight. So you keep that hoodoo with you."

"What fight?"

"I reckon you know. And if you don't, I reckon you're smart enough to recognize it when it finds you."

I shivered.

"Poppy, I'm so sorry about this." Knox stood at my side. "Let's go." His hand closed on my elbow and he guided me to the stairs.

I stopped and looked back at the woman. Her eyes were shut, and a small secretive smile curled her lips.

He rested his palm against the small of my back and pushed gently. "Let's go."

Knox hurried me down the stairs—away from the woman, away from Muriel's.

I paused in the square and drew a deep breath of humid air into my lungs. "Who was that woman?"

"Mama Vielle."

I waited for more.

"She says she's a Voodoo priestess." Knox's voice said he had his doubts.

"She's disturbing." An understatement.

"And you already had a disturbing day. I'm so sorry that happened."

"Not your fault."

I took another breath and looked around the square. Couples strolled. A saxophone player spun plaintive notes—they hung in the air, beautiful and fragile as glass ornaments on a Christmas tree. A line of people snaked out from under a green and white awning.

I smelled fried dough, and chicory, and the river.

"You should throw that thing away." Knox pointed at the bit of linen in my fingers. "Here, I'll do it." He held out his hand. Waiting.

I was tired of Knox Arnaut taking charge. I shook my head and dropped Mama Vielle's bit of hoodoo in my bag. "I will. Later."

He scowled. "May I see you home?"

"Thank you, but there's no need. Where can I find a cab?"

"There's a hotel half a block away. We'll get a bellman to call a taxi."

I LEANED my head against the backseat of the cab and hoped, for Adele's sake, that Carter Arnaut was less bossy than his cousin. The man had actually tried to climb in the cab with me. Some foolishness about seeing me safely to my door. I'd sent him on his way with a kiss on his cheek and a promise to see him soon.

I closed my eyes. "What is that you're listening to?"

"Boozoo Chavis," the cabbie replied.

"Who?" Boozoo was playing an accordion with verve.

"'Round these parts he's a Zydeco legend."

I'd have to take the cabbie's word for it. I turned my head and looked out the window at the crowded banquette. "What street are we on?"

"Chartres."

The people on the sidewalk were moving faster than the cab.

The traffic eased, the cabbie shot forward, and the faces flew by me. I spotted a face I recognized.

"Stop the cab!"

"What?"

"Stop the cab. I'm getting out!" I dropped a twenty over the front seat and opened the door. I'd seen him—the man who'd been chasing Vic Klein.

On the sidewalk—the banquette—I pulled my cell out my bag and said a silent *thank you* that I'd had the foresight to throw Detective Langlois' card in my bag. I stopped under a streetlight and punched in his number.

The man walked past me.

As soon as the phone rang, I walked, following half a block behind the man who'd been on the veranda at the Columns.

"Hello."

"It's Poppy Fields," I whispered.

"What's wrong, Miss Fields?"

"I saw him."

"Saw who?"

"The man who was following Vic Klein. The one who chased him into the Columns. He's walking down Chartres."

"What are you doing?"

"Walking down Chartres."

"Stop doing that."

"What? Why?"

"Because I don't want you to get shot."

"I won't. He's turning."

"Stop following him!"

Not happening. "He's turning on—" I peered up at the street sign "—Dumaine."

"Miss Fields!"

"What? Are you sending help or not?"

Detective Langlois sighed. "Is he walking to or from the river?"

"Which way is the river?"

The question earned me another sigh.

"This is too dangerous. Stop following him, Miss Fields."

"No." I skirted a mound of trash. "He doesn't know I'm back here. I'm fine." As long as I didn't trip on a crack and break my neck. These shoes were not made for walking in New Orleans. When I went to Saks, I'd buy flats. "He turned left. Does that help?"

"Away from the river." Whatever. "Is he alone?"

"Yes." I rounded the corner onto Dumaine.

"What's he wearing?"

Pants. "I don't know. When I saw his face, I hopped out of a cab. I didn't pay attention to his clothes."

"Did he see you?"

"No." Why would he notice a woman getting out of a cab? I was certain the man was unaware I was behind him.

"You're certain?"

Something cold and sharp settled near the small of my back and a hand gripped my arm.

My heart leapt to the upper regions of my chest and I swallowed a Langlois-was-right gasp.

"Give me your purse."

Seriously? A mugger? Now? My heart thudded back to its normal place. "You're kidding."

"Do I sound like I'm kidding?" asked Langlois.

"I wasn't talking to you." If I hadn't been concentrating on the man I was following, the cracks in the sidewalk, and talking on the phone, I'd have sensed the mugger's approach. Maybe.

"Your purse. Now." The guy with the knife in my back sounded as if he were from Brooklyn.

"Who are you talking to?" Detective Langlois demanded.

"The guy who's mugging me."

"You're kidding."

Exactly my response. "Nope."

"Now!" The tip of the knife dug deeper into my back. If he broke skin, he'd ruin my dress.

"Take it." The purse, a nothing-special clutch, held less than two hundred dollars cash, a lipstick, and some breath mints. Nothing worth getting stabbed for.

Keeping the knife pressed against my back, the mugger let go of my arm, grabbed the bag, and peered into it. "No credit cards?"

"You wanted to go shopping?"

The knife dug deeper. "Shut the hell up."

Down the street, the man from the Columns was two blocks away and turning. I was going to lose him. With a silent thank you to my father for years of Krav Maga lessons, I sank the too-high heel of my Louboutin into the mugger's insole and jabbed my elbow backward.

"*Ooomph.*"

The sharp bite of the knife blade at my back disappeared. The knife fell, and metal meeting paving stones made a hollow sound.

With the knife gone, I spun, raising my knee.

"Miss Fields, are you there?"

"Hold on." I kneed the mugger in the balls.

"*Ooomph.*" He joined his knife on the pavement—his fingers only inches away from the handle. That wasn't good.

"Miss Fields!" The voice boomed from my phone.

"Hold on." I kicked the knife into the street and lifted the cell to my ear. "What? I'm here."

"What is happening?"

"I disarmed the mugger." I looked down at the man on the sidewalk—the banquette. He wore black cargo pants, sneakers, and a ripped Saints t-shirt. His face, marred by a puckered scar that ran from the corner of his brow to the juncture of his chin and neck, was frozen in a rictus of pain.

"You and me, Miss Fields, we need to talk."

"Fine. Later." I reclaimed my bag.

"Put me on speaker."

"What? Why?"

"Just do it, Miss Fields."

I touched an icon and Detective Langlois' voice boomed into the street. "If anything happens to the woman you just assaulted, I'll make it my mission to see you spend the next ten years of your life in Angola. Do you understand?"

The mugger, who'd brought his knees up to his chin, nodded.

"He understands." I left the mugger on the pavement and trotted down the street toward the corner where Columns-man had turned.

"You're still following him, aren't you?"

"Hold on." I took Detective Langlois off speaker. "Yes. He turned right on—" I glanced up at the street sign "—Burgundy Street."

"Bur-*Gun*-dy."

"Seriously? You're correcting my pronunciation?" I rounded the corner and found a street filled with one- and two-story buildings painted in shades of gray by the thick night. The flare of streetlights revealed patches of actual paint color—lemon chiffon, deep salmon, and turquoise suitable for a Tiffany's box. The lights did not reveal a man. "He's gone."

"Thank God for that. Don't move."

"What?"

"You heard me." Detective Langlois sounded like a man who'd had his last nerve poked with a cattle prod.

"But—"

"Miss Fields, if you take another step, I'll have you arrested for assault."

That was too much. "Me? Assault?"

"You heard me."

"Who?"

"Did you, or did you not, just leave a man clutching his junk in the gutter?"

His question did not deserve an answer. "You'd really arrest me?"

"Pete Coombs will have my head if you get yourself killed. Now, don't move. I'm sending a car."

There was no way to tell which building Columns-man had entered. "Fine. I won't move. What is this street?"

"It's mostly residential."

Which meant Columns-man lived here, or had a friend who did. I took a few steps.

"Miss Fields." Detective Langlois interrupted my thoughts and my forward progress. "This is not your problem. You're in New Orleans to look pretty standing at the altar with Adele Coombs when she gets married next Saturday." He chuckled. "How ugly is your dress?"

"Pardon me?"

"How ugly is your dress?"

Bright and ruffled, the dress ticked off two out of Adele's four dress-like-a-southern-woman criteria. "It's not something I'd pick."

Now Langlois laughed out loud. "I don't know if they do it on purpose or not, but I've never met a bride who didn't pick ugly dresses for the women standing next to her."

Down the street, a door opened, and a man stepped onto the banquette.

"I see someone." I moved toward the figure

"Miss Fields—" Langlois' voice was a warning.

What could checking on who it was possibly hurt? "But—"

"Trust me, Miss Fields." All the laughter fled from Detective Langlois' voice. Instead he sounded as serious—as dangerous—as that Emily Blunt movie about Mexican drug smuggling. "You do not want to spend the night in a New Orleans jail."

Chapter Five

One of New Orleans' blue and white police cars pulled up next to me and a well-padded officer got out of the car and offered up a reassuring smile. "Miss Fields? I'm Frank Dupree. I'm here to take you home."

I glanced down the street. The man exiting the house had disappeared amongst the pedestrians who strolled the banquette.

The man from the Columns wasn't my problem—not really. I needed to remember that. Plus, Detective Langlois had threatened to have me arrested if I pursued him. Finally, there was the not-small issue of what I would do with a man who led six-man hit teams through the daylit streets of New Orleans when I caught up with him. All good reasons not to follow. Still I searched the walkers on the banquette, trying to pick out the right man.

"There's a blue and white beside you, Miss Fields. Get in the car." Detective Langlois' voice boomed from my cell, startling me. The man was incredibly annoying.

"Fine." It wasn't like I could spot Columns-guy in the dark.

"Good night, Detective." I hung up the phone with a vicious jab of my finger.

Officer Dupree opened the passenger door for me. "You're the woman who shot the guy fixing to kill Bill?" There was so much disbelief on his face—I might as well have been Uma Thurman. In a yellow track suit. Carrying a samurai sword.

"Bill?"

"Officer Wells."

The police officer who'd been shot after I wrecked Adele's Porsche. "How is he?"

"He'll be fine. Thanks to you." He nodded toward the empty seat. "Where can I take you?"

I gave him James's address and he whistled through his teeth. "Nice place."

"You know it?"

"Never been inside. It's a historic house—most of 'em in the French Quarter are. I heard tell it's haunted. You seen any ghosts?"

Did everyone in New Orleans believe in ghosts? "Not yet." I settled into the cruiser and surveyed the dashboard.

Officer Dupree closed the door, climbed into the driver's seat, and started the car.

"Have the police learned anything more about the shooting today?" I asked.

"The guy your friend took to the hospital—Sam Martin—he's going to make it."

"Thank God." Adele would have been devastated if he died after she tried so hard to save him. "What happened?"

"What do you mean?"

"Why was there a rolling gun battle on St. Charles?"

"That information is above my paygrade, Miss Fields."

I turned on one of Chariss's gets-them-every-time smiles. "I bet you've heard something."

An answering smile flickered across his lips. "Vic Klein, the guy you killed—"

My heart squeezed and my intestines cringed—I'd killed a man. I glanced down at my lap and tried—tried hard—not to let the emotion welling inside me reflect on my face. "What about him?"

"Word is he stepped on the wrong toes. Could be he was moving product through the port. Could be someone wanted in on the action."

"The action?"

"Heroin, coke, you name it." The policeman pulled away from the curb.

"The man who was chasing him is somewhere nearby." I tapped on the window. "He might even be on the sidewalk—the banquette—right now."

"Not your problem, Miss Fields." Officer Dupree sounded an awful lot like Detective Langlois.

I peered out the window, searching for the right face in the dark. "You could be the one to catch him."

The policeman chuckled and turned right at the next corner. "If it's all the same to you, I'll leave the drug kingpins to the men who're trained to go after 'em."

When my dad died, I moved to Hollywood and lived with my mom. And in Hollywood, producers knew perception was reality. Heroes were handsome. Villains were dastardly. "He didn't look like a drug kingpin."

"What does a kingpin look like?"

"Al Pacino in *Scarface*?"

He laughed. "Could be you're right. Could be kingpins look like everyone else."

The man on the veranda had looked more like a waiter than Al Pacino. I swallowed a sigh and leaned back against the cracked leather seat. "Are there gangs in New Orleans?"

"Yeah."

"MS-13, Crips, Bloods?" I'd officially run out of gang names.

"Nah. They tried to move in, but our boys took 'em out. We have our own gangs—3nG, Byrds, Magnolia Boys. Things are different in New Orleans. Most gangs, there's a hierarchy. Not here. In New Orleans, gang structure is loose, and the gangs are more dangerous."

"What do you mean?"

"In a structured gang, the leaders don't want the police in their business. The leaders keep the rank and file from killing bystanders. You don't have that in New Orleans. Here, it's every man for himself. Anarchy." He shifted his gaze from the road to me. "Why do you want to know?"

"Aren't gangs used to distribute drugs?"

"Yeah. But what happened on St. Charles—it's not related to street gangs. You got big shipments coming through the port—they're going elsewhere. Atlanta. Charlotte. St. Louis. Bigger cities."

"Does what happened at the Columns happen often?"

He shifted his gaze back to the street. "I wouldn't go that far."

"The man I killed, Vic Klein—" I took a deep I-didn't-have-a-choice breath "—was he associated with a gang?"

"Nah." The policeman glanced my way, even offered me a sympathetic grin—almost as if he understood shooting someone, no matter the reason, was gut-wrenching. "If there was still organized crime in New Orleans, I'd say Vic would've had his hand in that."

"No organized crime?"

"Not since Carlos Marcello died."

"Who is Carlos Marcello?"

"The last big boss."

"How long has he been gone?"

"Going on thirty years."

So Vic Klein wasn't in a gang. Wasn't associated with organized crime. "You're telling me a man with no local ties moves to New Orleans and starts moving product through the port. Easy as that?"

"Looked that way. But maybe we were wrong about Vic. We had plenty of suspicions, but whenever the DEA raided his shipments, they came up empty. Didn't find a thing. Vic always came off clean as a whistle."

"If he was clean, he wouldn't have been in that shoot-out on St. Charles. He wouldn't have put a gun to my head."

"There's that," Officer Dupree ceded.

"Maybe someone tipped him off? About the raids?"

He shrugged. "Anything's possible."

"What if—"

"You know what, Miss Fields?"

"What?"

"This is Detective Langlois's problem. Not yours."

I laced my fingers together and tapped my hands against my nose. This made no sense. "A stranger figured out who to pay off at the port, figured out how to move product without the police or the DEA catching on, figured out how to move the product out of New Orleans without getting caught. All without any local help?"

Officer Dupree's eyes narrowed and the friendly slipped off his face—now he looked worried. "You seem like a nice girl."

"Thank you."

"Too nice to be involved with all this. So take my advice. Stay away from anything to do with Vic Klein."

"But—"

"You ask a lot of questions."

"I'm curious."

"It would be a shame for you to get hurt."

I opened my mouth, but no words came out.

"We're here." Seemingly unconcerned with the cars behind him, Officer Dupree stopped the car and put it in park. Then he opened his door and hurried around the side of the car and opened mine.

"Who do you think was helping Vic Klein?" I stepped onto the banquette.

"Trust me, Miss Fields. You want to stay out of this."

"Who?" I insisted.

He shook his head and sealed his lips. He would say no more.

I'd have to find the information another way. "Thank you for the ride." I glanced up at James's house. "And the conversation."

"Any time, Miss Fields. NOPD owes you one." He ignored the line of cars backing up behind his cruiser. "I'll see you inside."

I rang the bell. "Ladybug, the housekeeper, will let me in. No need to back up traffic."

He glanced at the traffic jam he'd caused and shrugged. "I reckon Detective Langlois will want to know you're safely home."

"I'm fine." I glanced at the growing line of cars. "Truly. I promise I'll go right inside."

A horn blared.

Officer Dupree crossed his arms and offered me a bland smile. He wasn't going anywhere until I was in the house.

We waited long seconds.

Finally, Ladybug opened the door. "Miss Fields—" she saw Officer Dupree and her brows rose to her hairline "—is everything all right?"

"Fine, thank you." I smiled up at the waiting police officer. "Thanks again for the ride, Officer Dupree."

He nodded at me and returned to his cruiser.

I stepped inside James's home but paused in the foyer when my cell vibrated. I dug it out of my bag and looked at the screen. I could ignore the call. It had been a long day, a long evening. Exhaustion nipped at my heels. But if I ignored him, he'd keep calling or—worse—show up. I touched the screen. "Hello."

"What the hell is going on?"

"Hello, Jake."

"I thought you were going to New Orleans for a wedding."

"*Yip!*"

I bent down and scooped Consuela into my arms. "I did. That's why I'm here." Not that I owed Jake, the man who'd broken my heart, an explanation.

"I heard you shot someone."

News traveled fast. "Yes," I allowed.

"You can't stay out of trouble for five minutes. Are you in danger?"

"Do you need anything else, Miss Fields?" Ladybug spoke softly.

"No. Thank you."

"Thank me for what?" Jake snapped.

I wasn't doing it again. I was not carrying on two conversations at the same time. "Hold on, Jake." I held the phone away from my ear. "Thanks so much for letting me in, Ladybug."

"You're welcome. If you don't need me, I'll say good night." She nodded and disappeared toward the back of the house.

Which left me with Jake. I took a deep breath. "I'm back."

"You should go home to California."

Just who did he think he was? "I'm in Adele's wedding. I'm not going anywhere."

"It's not safe for you there. What if Diaz comes after you?"

"Not your problem."

"*Yip*." Consuela agreed with me.

The sound that came through my phone was somewhere between a splutter and a snort. "It is too my problem. You're being stupid."

"*Grrr*."

I agreed with the dog in my arms. "The only thing I've ever been stupid over is you." Totally not true—but Jake didn't need to know that. "And I'm much smarter now."

"What if Diaz sends someone to kill you?"

It was my sincere hope Diaz was taking an I-hope-she-dies attitude rather than a make-sure-she-dies view on the matter. "Mark Stone arrives tomorrow."

Another splutter-snort. A splort?

"And I can take care of myself."

"That's it. I'm coming to New Orleans."

"What? Why? Don't!"

"Someone has to take care of you."

"Yes, someone does. Me. And it's extremely insulting that you don't think I'm up to it."

That he answered with a few seconds' worth of silence. "Poppy." His voice was as honeyed and warm as a star-filled southern night. If he couldn't bully me, he'd charm me.

"Don't *Poppy* me."

"What do you mean?" Now he sounded innocent, as if he had no idea why I objected to my name being used as a verbal caress.

"I'm hanging up now."

"Yip." Consuela approved.

"Wait!"

"What, Jake?"

"Promise me you'll be careful."

"I'm always careful."

The last thing I heard as I hung up the phone was another splort.

I closed my eyes and dropped a kiss onto the top of Consuela's head.

"*Grrr.*"

Consuela didn't usually growl at my kisses. "What is it?

"*Grrr.*"

The feeling of something about to happen was as real as the parquet floor beneath my feet. Someone was watching me.

My heart stuttered and I completed a slow circle. I was alone.

"*Grrr.*"

Footsteps came from the dark room across the hall.

"Ladybug?" It couldn't be Ladybug. I'd watched Ladybug retreat to the back of the house. Still, with a dry mouth, I called again, "Ladybug?"

There was no answer.

"*Grrr.*" The hair on Consuela's back stood straight up.

"Ladybug?" I tiptoed toward the dark room with my pulse beating in my ears. "Is that you?" It couldn't be.

The footsteps halted.

A chill skittered down my neck and my fingers were suddenly clammy. I hugged Consuela close. "Ladybug?"

There was no answer.

With my free hand, I groped inside the door and flipped the light switch.

The room was filled with enormous leather seats and an even more enormous television screen. And there was no in it. No one. Just the sudden brightness of the overhead lights and a smudge of darkness hovering in the farthest corner.

"Ladybug?" My voice was a raw whisper.

"*Grrr.*" Consuela would protect me from the smudge.

The phone in my pocket vibrated and I jumped. My fingers shook, but I swiped the right button. "Hello."

"Poppy, it's me."

"Hi." My breath had gone missing.

"What's wrong?" Thor's voice took on a concerned edge.

"Nothing."

"You're sure?" He wasn't convinced.

"Really, it was nothing. I thought I heard something." I ignored the smudge and crossed to the French doors that opened onto a narrow balcony. "I was wrong." Pressing the phone to my shoulder, I peeked behind the drapes. Nothing. Nor was there anyone lurking outside.

"You sound odd."

"Do I?" Had I imagined the footsteps? I opened the door and looked down into Royal Street. Nothing seemed amiss. "I'm fine."

Thor did not reply.

"When will you get in?" I asked.

"My plane just landed."

A breath of cold air tickled my neck and I glanced over my shoulder. The room was still empty. "You're in New Orleans?"

"I was in Houston. I caught a flight."

"Do you know the address?"

"Got it."

"Call when you get here. I'll let you in." Where had the footsteps come from? No matter what I'd told Thor, I knew what I'd heard—the quick light steps of a woman. In this room. But the door I'd used to enter was the only way in or out. And the room was empty.

Carefully, I locked the door to the balcony and backed out of James's theater. I was unwilling to linger another second in a room where unexplained footsteps still echoed in my ears.

Officer Dupree had said James's house was haunted.

For tonight, I believed him. The thought of Thor sharing my roof was comforting. The thought of telling Thor my fears left me red-faced with embarrassment.

In the living room, Consuela and I settled onto to the couch. The one that faced the entrance.

She circled three times, then tucked herself into a small fluffy ball.

I picked up the newspaper and—desperate not to think about the footsteps in the empty room across the hall—scanned the headlines. The Port of New Orleans had closed a real estate deal that gave it control of a railroad.

The Port. Again.

If Vic Klein had no involvement with gangs or organized crime, who was making it possible for him to bring drugs through the port? And how were the drugs being moved once they arrived?

I stood. "I'm gonna grab my laptop." My voice was hardly a murmur.

Consuela opened one eye but didn't move.

Nor did she move when I returned. Instead, she snored softly.

I sat next to her and pulled up the Port of New Orleans' website. There was a strategic plan. There were parking instructions for cruise passengers. There were links to shopping and dining on the River Walk. There were plans for economic development. There were maps. There were portals for shippers to track containers. There was a wedding reception venue.

There was no explanation of how Vic had moved drugs. I hadn't expected one.

Now that Vic was dead, what would happen to his business? Were his containers still sitting on the dock?

"*Grrr*." Even in her sleep, Consuela thought that Vic and his drugs were not my problem.

"But—"

"*Grrr.*"

My cell rang, and Consuela opened her eyes and lifted her head from her paws.

"Hello." Why was I whispering?

"I'm here."

A heretofore unnoticed tightness in the back of my neck loosened and I hauled myself up from the comfort of James's couch. "I'll let you in."

I hung up, dropped the phone onto a cushion, and hurried to the front door.

Consuela came with—her nails clicked on the parquet.

I yanked open the door and a smile stretched my lips. "I'm glad you're here."

Thor didn't smile. Instead he pushed through the door, closing it as soon as he was inside. "Poppy, what the hell is going on?"

"What do you mean?"

"I was followed from the airport."

"*Yip.*" Consuela didn't care who'd followed him, she wanted a greeting.

I scooped her up and Thor scratched behind her ears.

"Who followed you?"

"I thought maybe you could tell me."

"No idea. No one knows you're coming." I led him toward the living room. "Are you sure this isn't part of whatever it is you're working on?"

He shrugged.

"What did they look like?"

"I just saw headlights."

If it were anyone else, I might have argued—headlights are headlights. But if Thor said he'd been followed, he'd been followed.

I deposited Consuela on the couch, reached for my phone, and froze.

The cell I'd dropped on a cushion wasn't where I'd left it. Instead, it rested next to my laptop on the coffee table.

A shiver trickled down my spine. What in the world was going on?

Chapter Six

Canal Street's banquette was crowded with slow-moving tourists, hungover street people (quite possibly the tourists were hungover too), and men pushing bright yellow trash barrels. Some of the cleanup men speared crumpled fast-food wrappers. Others swept up cigarette butts. The air smelled of last night's liquor and the river.

None of that mattered.

Nor did drug dealers, killers, or unexplained footsteps in the night.

Phones might move by themselves. Jake might threaten to descend upon New Orleans like some Old Testament plague.

It didn't matter.

I walked with a smile on my face. My name had not been mentioned in the coverage of the shooting that ran on *The Times-Picayune*'s front page. Not even a hint. I owed Pete Coombs a huge thank you.

Plus, shopping at Saks—at a Saks within walking distance. A spring livened my step.

I floated through Saks' doors into a cloud of perfumed air.

"Good morning. May I help you?" An attractive woman with a helmet of white hair stood just inside the double glass doors. Her sharp blue eyes took in my Hermès bag, my Tod's loafers, and the locket at my neck.

I took in the chic cut of her blouse. "I was told to ask for Lillian."

"I'm Lillian."

"I'm Poppy Fields. Ladybug said you'd be able to help me with some clothes for a wedding."

"Ladybug Jenkins? How kind of her." Lillian tilted her well-coiffed head. "I'd be delighted to help you. Do you have any favorite designers?"

"That's the problem. Ladybug says my clothes are all wrong."

"What are you dressing for?"

"Today there's lunch at Galatoire's and a supper party. Tomorrow there's a picnic at Audubon Park. Then there are more lunches and cocktail parties and dinners. Next Friday, there's the rehearsal dinner, and there's a brunch the day after the wedding."

"Whose wedding?"

"Adele Coombs."

"Ah." That one syllable said so much.

Lillian showed me ladylike shoes with chunky heels that wouldn't get caught in the cracks in the banquette. She put me in flowered dresses and skirts with hems that brushed my knees. She sold me whisper-thin cardigan sweaters and silk blouses. She talked me into a cocktail dress that reminded me of an orchid and an evening suit (wasn't I too young?) the color of forget-me-nots. Escada. Jason Wu. Pucci. Erdem. Carolina Herrera. Lela Rose.

Through it all, Lillian kept up a running commentary. "That

blouse is fabulous, but I'm not sure about the skirt. Have you been to the aquarium? You must go while you're here. Try this skirt instead." She pressed an Altuzza skirt into my hands. "And Frenchmen Street. Do you like music? You must go to Frenchmen Street." She narrowed her eyes when I emerged from the dressing room. "See? I was right. That skirt is much better. Do you like art? We have wonderful galleries. You're staying at Mr. Ballester's? That's how you know Ladybug? You're in luck. M.S Rau is so close to you. You must go and you must ask to see the secret room."

"The secret room?"

Lillian nodded. "Walking into the secret room is like walking into a museum where everything is for sale. The last time I was there, there was a Monet hanging on the wall and a Rodin on a pedestal in the middle of the room."

"M.S. Rau's?"

"Tell them I sent you."

I looked up from smoothing the silk skirt she'd pressed into my hands and stared at her.

She flushed. "No kick-backs. I promise. I just think you'd enjoy it."

After an hour, I'd accumulated enough clothing to see me through three southern weddings. "I believe I'll wear that." I pointed to a demure Valentino. "With those Jimmy Choo pumps. Would you please have the rest delivered to James Ballester's house?"

Lillian opened her mouth as if she were about to tell me Saks didn't deliver. "I'll take everything myself."

"Thank you." I signed the sales receipt and called Thor, who'd stayed at James's house—inexplicably, he hadn't wanted to come shopping with me. "I'm ready."

"I'll be there in five minutes."

A thought occurred to me. "What are you wearing?"

There was a long uncomfortable pause. "What do you mean?"

"What are you wearing?" I insisted. Thor was many things. Strong. Brave. Handsome. But well-dressed, he was not.

"Pants, Poppy. I'm wearing pants."

"And what else?"

"A shirt."

"We need to get you a few things."

"What? No."

"Yes."

I turned away from Lillian and lowered my voice. "Think of it as going undercover."

"No."

"Yes." I could out-stubborn him and we both knew it.

"Fine."

"Come to Saks. I'll be waiting."

A few minutes later, Thor strode past the perfume counter with thunder writ across his face.

Lillian took only a moment to get over the arrival of a Norse god. In no time, she had him in pressed khakis (*we'll hem them while you wait*), a crisp cotton shirt, a shell-pink bowtie (*the little starfish are very masculine, I promise*), and a navy blazer (*aren't you lucky you can buy off the rack?*). She even had his feet in a pair of bucks.

Thor looked ready to smite her. And me.

Especially when we made him try on and buy a Brioni suit.

He insisted on buying his own clothes and visibly paled when he saw the total (Brioni doesn't come cheap).

"I feel ridiculous." He fiddled with his starfish bowtie as we walked toward Galatoire's.

He didn't look ridiculous. He looked—I stared into a store window. "You look nice."

"Who are we having lunch with?"

"My friend Adele and her fiancé, Carter, Adele's parents, and Carter's cousin, Knox."

"Do they know I'm coming?"

"Yes."

"What did you tell them?"

"You're my boyfriend and we've been missing each other so much you decided to surprise me."

The phone call to Adele had been tricky. "Are you okay?" I'd asked.

"Just tired. I stayed late at the hospital."

"How's Mr. Martin?"

"He's okay." Her voice sounded the same way it did when she'd had a term paper due or pulled an all-nighter studying for a test. Exhausted. It was easy to picture her rubbing the bridge of her nose. "How did you know his name?"

I *so* didn't want to tell her about my drive home in a police car after I'd ditched her fiancé's cousin. "Detective Langlois must have mentioned it. Um, Adele..."

"Yes?" Now she sounded wary.

"My boyfriend flew in."

"Your boyfriend? Jake?"

Ouch. "No. I haven't been with Jake for a while."

"Then who?"

"Mark. His name is Mark Stone."

"You've never mentioned him. How did you meet?"

Telling her Mr. Brown had sent him to protect me in Paris was not a good answer—she might ask who Mr. Brown was. And *that* would prompt still more questions. "A friend introduced us."

"How long is he in town?"

"I don't know."

"Why haven't I heard about him?"

"We just recently took things to the next level."

"And he followed you here? I don't know if that's romantic or creepy."

"When you meet him, you'll think it's romantic."

"If you say so." She hadn't sounded convinced.

I peeked at Thor out of the corner of my eye. He looked like a cover model for *Garden and Gun*. Adele would definitely think his arrival was romantic.

We turned right on Bourbon Street and Thor glanced over his shoulder.

"Are you still being followed?"

"Yes."

"How can you tell?" I refrained—barely—from swiveling my head and studying the crowded banquette behind us.

"I can tell."

"We need to talk about this."

Thor's lips thinned to nothing.

But the who's-following-Thor discussion would have to wait. We'd arrived. "That must be the line." I pointed to a snarl of people on the banquette.

"The line?"

"I'm told Galatoire's doesn't take reservations for its downstairs dining room. There are no exceptions." The people who'd been paid to wait had brought lawn chairs. Everyone else stood.

Adele waited for us by the front door. "There you are." She took my elbow and looked up at Thor with wide eyes. "You must be Mark. We're so glad you could join us." She led us into a long narrow room. Black and white tile peppered the floor. Dark green wallpaper decorated with gold fleurs-de-lis reached for an impossibly high ceiling. Lazy overhead fans stirred the air. "Come meet everyone."

Introductions were made.

Cheeks were kissed.

Not Knox's. He was too busy scowling. First at Thor then at me.

Pete Coombs swallowed me in an enormous hug and whispered in my ear, "Thank you for yesterday."

"Thank you for keeping me out of the paper."

"It was nothing."

I doubted that.

Thor pulled out my chair.

We sat.

A waiter took our drink order and put menus in our waiting hands.

I ordered a salad. I had no choice. The alternative was exchanging my new clothes for larger sizes.

Pete frowned at me. "Mineral water and a salad? You'll waste away to nothing."

"Leave her alone, Daddy." Adele had also ordered a salad.

Pete turned his attention to Mark, who'd ordered some kind of bourbon I'd never heard of and Crab Sardou. "Where are you from, Mark?"

"Bentonville."

"Bentonville?" Adele's mother, Patrice, loaded a lot into the name of a town. "Do you know CeeCee and Jimmy Burke?"

"Friends of my parents."

Patrice smiled as if Thor had passed some kind of test.

"Bentonville?" Knox rubbed his chin. "Does someone work for Walmart?"

"My father."

"Greeter?"

"Chief Information Officer."

Pete leaned back in his chair. "Are you a Razorback?"

"No, sir. I went to Yale."

"Call me Pete." Apparently Thor had passed Pete's test as well.

Truth was, I'd learned more about Thor in five minutes with Adele's family than I'd learned in all the days we spent together in Paris. I'd never asked where he was from or where he went to school. If I'd thought about his family, I'd have assumed his father was Odin, not an IT guy.

Pete, who'd decided to try Thor's brand of bourbon, took a sip of his drink and nodded his approval. "What do you do, Mark?"

"Daddy, stop being so nosy." Adele's smile traveled the table, then she patted the back of Thor's hand. "You can't imagine all the questions he asked Carter when we started dating—" she waited a beat "—and he's known Carter since he was a gleam in his daddy's eye."

"I'm protective," Peter replied. "And Poppy did save you yesterday."

"That doesn't give you free rein in her personal life."

I turned to Knox. "Have the police learned anything more about the shooting?"

"Let's not talk about that." Patrice's hands fluttered above the table. "So upsetting. Mark, have you been to New Or—"

"Excuse me."

We all shifted our attention to a woman in a Lilly Pulitzer shift.

The men stood.

"Please, sit down." The woman (pretty, blonde, thin) pushed her manicured hands down on imaginary shoulders as if the motion could return the men to their seats.

"Delia, how nice to see you." Patrice's narrowed eyes and a tightness near her lips told me she didn't mean a word.

No one seemed inclined to make introductions.

"I'm sorry to interrupt your lunch, but we're having a debate." Delia glanced back at a table populated by three women as blonde and thin as her.

"About?" asked Adele.

"Are you Poppy Fields?"

"I am."

Delia shifted her gaze to Thor. "Are you Chris Hemsworth?"

"No," Adele replied. "He's not."

"I knew it. I knew he'd never step out on his wife."

"Mark Stone." Thor extended his hand.

"Mark is attending the wedding with Poppy. They're together." Icicles hung from Patrice's voice.

Delia did not reply. Or move. She merely stared up at Thor with her hand still hanging limply in his.

Awkward.

"The waiter is serving your salad, dear." Patrice Coombs's bad side (and Delia was definitely on it) sounded like a very chilly place to be.

Delia shook her head. "Pardon?"

"Your salad." Patrice inclined her chin toward the table where Delia's friends waited. "Your meal is being served."

"Oh. Right. Sorry to interrupt. Nice to meet you, Mark." She looked up at Thor with eyes as blue as an October sky.

Thor took back his hand. "Nice meeting you too."

Delia returned to her table in a daze.

"Sorry about that," said Patrice as the men resumed their seats.

I cast a quick glance at Delia's table. She was recounting something to her friends and smiling at Thor as if he actually were Chris Hemsworth. "Must be the tie. The saleswoman said starfish were very masculine."

Adele giggled. "She was right."

Lunch was delicious. And loud. And being in the dining room, where the Coombs knew everyone, was like being at a party.

Three hours after we sat down, Knox looked at his watch and murmured something about getting back to work.

Pete insisted on picking up the check.

When Thor and I emerged onto the bright banquette, I blinked and linked my arm through his. "Is your shadow still with us?"

"Let's walk." He led me away from Canal Street.

"So this guy who's following you—"

"What about him?"

"Who is he?"

"No idea. I noticed him at the airport. He's been with me since."

"Guess," I insisted.

Thor rubbed his chin. "You've heard of Venti?"

"Yes." Venti was a potentially deadly party drug. "I thought the Sinaloans had given up on it."

"No. I was in Texas tracing shipments."

"What did you find?"

"They're using ports."

We walked past a club advertising nude showgirls. An almost-nude showgirl pressed a flyer into Thor's hands.

She didn't seem to notice my glare. "Let's get off Bourbon Street."

We took the next right and our steps slowed.

"Ports? Like the Port of New Orleans?"

"Yeah, ports."

"Don't officials from the ports check the containers? Wouldn't they notice all those pills?"

"The drug-sniffing dogs don't know what to sniff for. The officials don't know what to look for. We do know, so far, containers have come through Galveston, San Diego, Miami, and New Orleans."

New Orleans.

"But someone picked you up at the airport, right? How did they know you were coming?"

Thor's face turned grim. "No idea."

I paused and peered into a shop. Open doors revealed a disturbing jumble of beads and masks and Tarot cards, Madonnas and skeletons, potions and powders, burlap dolls and black candles. I stepped back and looked at the sign hanging above the door. A Voodoo shop. Voodoo. Like the charm tucked into one of the inner pockets of my handbag. I shuddered and resumed walking. "Do you think what happened yesterday—the shooting—has something to do with Venti?"

"Yeah."

"But the police think Klein worked for the Sinaloans."

"Maybe someone wanted to hijack the shipment. Getting in on the ground floor with a new drug could be worth billions."

"He wanted me to take him to the port."

"What?"

"When Klein was in the car with me—" not telling Thor about the gun at my head was only a small omission "—he wanted me to take him to the port. Do you think the containers are sitting on the dock already?"

"Maybe." Thor shoved his hands in his pockets. "Anything's possible."

We turned onto Royal Street.

"Is he still behind us?"

"Who?" Was Thor being deliberately obtuse?

"The guy tailing you."

"Yes."

"Shouldn't we—I don't know—lose him?"

"Why?"

"Because he's following us."

"Are you going to a secret rendezvous?"

"No."

"Then let him follow."

I scowled at him. "The containers on the dock—can't you insist they search them?"

"Who's they?"

"I don't know. Customs. Whoever's job it is to search containers."

"They don't know what to look for. A customs official could be looking right at the shipment and not recognize it. There was a shipment seized in California. The Venti was in little candy boxes. The pills looked like Altoids. They only found the drugs because they had a tip about what to look for." He shook his head. "Besides, do you have any idea how many containers arrive from Mexico every day?

"No."

"A lot. Without the name of the shipping company or some idea of what's inside the containers, it would be like looking for a needle in a haystack."

"How do we find the shipping company?"

"We? We don't. You have a wedding."

That didn't deserve a response. I gave him my best Medusa stare and waited.

And waited.

The silence between us stretched.

And stretched.

I rested my hand on his arm. "You know I'm not letting you do this alone."

"Fine. You win. Mr. Brown gave me a name."

I waited some more.

"Mason Hubbard."

"Never heard of him." Not that I'd expected to. "Where do we find him?"

"Frenchmen Street."

"The music street?"

"You've been there?"

"No. But Lillian told me about it." I pulled out my cell and glanced at the time. "We've got a few hours till the party. What are we waiting for?"

"Poppy—"

"If you think I'm going to sit quietly while you go to Frenchmen Street without me, you're crazy."

"He won't be there till later tonight."

I glanced at Thor's face. He looked shifty. "You're lying."

"I'd never lie to you."

"If I had a dollar for every time a man told me that, I'd never have to work again."

"You don't have to work now."

That was beside the point. "Don't lie to me, Mark. Please."

Thor stared at me for a long second, then nodded. "I'm not lying to you, Poppy. And I won't. He's not there. He goes on at ten."

"He's a musician?"

"Yeah."

"You were planning on going without me?"

"Yeah." At least he was being honest.

"Forget that. We're partners."

Chapter Seven

"How many people are attending this party?" Thor demanded.

It was a reasonable question. We'd been in line to be dropped off forever, and we were crammed in the back of the world's smallest taxi. Thor was folded like a pretzel; his knees grazed his chin. I refrained—barely—from pointing out that if we'd taken the streetcar, as I'd suggested, he'd be standing tall and we'd already have drinks in our hands. "Just a few hundred of their closest friends."

"At a house?"

I assumed this was a rhetorical question. We were in the Garden District—the houses weren't small.

"You do realize most people can't host hundreds of guests in their homes?"

"There must be a neighborhood like this one in Bentonville."

"Nope. There are large houses, but they're relatively new construction. Nothing like that." He tapped the window, indicating a Victorian mansion.

"It's not as if it's a seated dinner." I pointed at the invitation. "See? Cocktail buffet."

"What?"

"A cocktail buffet."

Thor grumbled something unintelligible.

"Pardon?"

"Who are the hosts?" Whatever he'd mumbled before, it wasn't a question about our hosts.

"Anne and Clay Geary. Adele told me Anne and Patrice have been friends since grade school."

The driver inched to a stop in front of a Georgian house lit up brighter than a Christmas tree.

Thor tossed a bill into the front seat and wrenched open the back door. "Let's get this over with."

"You make it sound as if I'm taking you for a tetanus shot." We had a week's worth of festivities before the actual wedding. If Thor was this crabby at all the events, the coming days would last forever. "This is a party. You might have fun."

"It's a party where we don't know anyone."

"Sometimes those are the best kind."

We strolled up the front walk and waiters holding trays of Champagne welcomed us. I took a glass and clinked its rim against the glass in Thor's hands. "We don't have to stay all night. We can leave in plenty of time to get to Frenchmen Street."

Thor looked at me as if I was speaking a language he didn't understand.

"To find Mason Hubbard," I added.

"I'll go to Frenchmen Street. You can go home and hang up your new clothes."

"We've already talked about this. Besides, Ladybug already hung up all my new clothes." I followed my ears and walked through an enormous front hall, straight back to a pair of

French doors opening onto a patio filled with lights and people and a jazz band. I paused in the doorway and wagged a finger at him. "You're not going to Frenchmen Street without me."

Thor's eyes flashed. Like lightning. "Poppy—"

"You look gorgeous!" Adele wrapped me in a warm hug, then rose up on her tiptoes and kissed Thor's cheek. "And you look very handsome."

Thor blushed.

"You're the one who looks gorgeous." I admired Adele's dress. "No one can outshine the bride."

"Ever." Carter appeared at her side. "Poppy—" he kissed my cheek "—Mark—" he shook Thor's hand "—sorry to steal her away, but Great Aunt Agnes wants to see her."

"Who?" Adele asked.

"Great Aunt Agnes. From Louisville."

Adele tilted her head. "The one who's rich and old and you're her favorite living relation?"

"That's the one."

"Say no more. Poppy, we'll talk later. Eat. Drink. Dance. Have fun."

Thor watched her float away with his mouth hanging open.

"She was kidding."

"What?"

"She was kidding about the rich aunt."

"Are you sure?"

"She is rich. She is an aunt. And she does raise horses in Kentucky. But Adele's not remotely interested in her money. She actually told me Aunt Agnes would be the most interesting woman at the wedding."

"That's only because she doesn't know your secrets."

I felt a tap on my shoulder and turned.

"Forgive me for interrupting, but you're Poppy Fields." A

dapper little man with stars in his eyes regarded me from behind horn-rimmed glasses.

I recognized the dazzled expression in the man's eyes. I braced myself for what was coming.

"Oh my stars, I hardly know what to say." The man held the tips of his fingers to his cheeks. "I'm a tremendous fan of your mother's." He extended his right hand. "Lamar Prentiss."

At least Lamar was clean and polite. Sometimes the people who demanded to meet me were neither. "A pleasure, Lamar. This is my friend, Mark Stone."

Lamar's gaze skipped over Mark as if my six-foot-something escort was invisible. "I can't believe you're actually here."

"I'm here." And I wished I wasn't. Having Chariss's fans fawn over me wasn't my favorite thing.

"You are! You are!" Lamar beamed at me. "When did you last see her?"

Her. Chariss. "When we were in Paris."

He held his hands over his heart. "When she saved the city?"

"She was very brave."

Next to me, Thor choked on his Champagne.

"Are you from New Orleans, Lamar?"

"A native."

"How do you know Adele and Carter?"

"I've known Carter since he was in high school."

"You're a teacher?"

"A lawyer. Carter got into a little—" Lamar measured little between his thumb and pointer finger "—scrape and his daddy hired me to get him out of it."

"Carter? In trouble? Do tell."

He shook his head and smiled as if Carter's secret was especially juicy. "Sorry, my dear. That's privileged."

I wrinkled my nose at him. "You can't tell Chariss Carlton's daughter?"

"Alas, no."

"I'll get it out of Adele."

"If she knows."

Adele knew. She and Carter were perfect for each other. They didn't keep secrets. "Lamar..."

"Yes, my dear."

I leaned forward and lowered my voice. "You seem like a man who knows everyone, and I know no one. Who should I meet at this party?"

"Everyone wants to meet Adele's famous friend. Take your pick."

"Yes, but who's interesting?"

"What are you interested in? Art? Music? The latest stock tips?"

"As it turns out—" I smiled at him with a flirty curl of the lips I borrowed from Chariss "—I'm interested in shipping."

"Shopping?"

"Shipping." I held my pointer finger to my lips. "Don't tell a soul, but I'm helping Chariss research a part."

"Really?" He was near breathless.

I nodded. And lied. "It's a film about drug smugglers and pirates and—" I glanced at Thor "—a secret agent."

"How exciting!"

"Is there anyone here who can tell me about the Port of New Orleans?"

"You know what? There is! I saw Lyman Cox not five minutes ago."

"And who is Lyman Cox?"

"He's on the Port board."

"How did he end up on the board?" asked Thor.

Lamar peered up at Thor as if he'd never seen someone so tall or so simple. "The governor appointed him."

"I'd love to meet him. But—" I shook my head and lowered my voice "—please don't tell him why. Let's keep quiet about Chariss's film—it's our secret."

He smirked and pressed a finger against his lips. He'd be telling everyone at the party he'd helped Chariss Carlton research a part within minutes. If anyone wondered about my sudden interest in the port, there was an easy reason readily available. Lamar offered me his arm.

I took it.

Thor followed us through the crowd of chattering people.

"There he is, under the lanai."

The swimming pool was filled with floating votives and the flickering light on the water was almost magical. On the far side, a bar was set up in an open-air cabana. "The tall man with the silver hair?"

"That's him."

Lyman Cox wasn't just tall with a thick thatch of to-die-for hair. He was handsome. A flock of women flitted around him.

Lamar paused mid-step. "I should warn you. Lyman has something of a reputation with the ladies."

"It's a good thing I brought Mark."

Thor splorted.

We skirted the swimming pool and sidled up to Lyman and his harem.

Lamar cleared his throat. "Lyman, I have someone you simply must meet."

Lyman's gaze shifted from a daringly displayed décolleté to Lamar and from Lamar to me. His eyes widened.

Sometimes looking exactly like my movie-star mother was useful.

Lyman extended his hand, taking mine. "Charmed."

Lyman Cox's hand was warm and rough and big. There was no reason his touch should make me feel cold. I shivered.

"This lovely young lady is Poppy Fields."

Lyman's silver brows rose.

"And this is her friend, Mark Stone."

Thor's expression was stony.

"Poppy, Mark, meet Lyman Cox."

"Pleased to meet you, Lyman." I gave him Chariss's best you'll-be-putty-in-my-hands smile.

"You must be one of Adele's friends."

"I am. It's such a thrill to be here in your beautiful city for her wedding."

"We're thrilled you're here."

"Tell me, what do you do, Lyman?"

"I work for a bank."

"Lyman is being modest." Lamar adjusted the tilt of his bowtie. "He's the majority shareholder in the bank and he's on the board of the Port of New Orleans."

"The port! You don't say. I've always loved ships." I rested my hand on Lyman's arm and pretended I didn't hear Thor gnashing his teeth. "You must tell me all about it."

Lyman glanced at my empty Champagne glass. "Lamar, Poppy needs another drink. Champagne?"

I nodded.

Lamar trotted off to the bar.

"You're probably thinking of yachts. As it happens, I keep a—"

"No, no." I didn't want to hear about his yacht. I wanted to hear about the port. "I think the port sounds fascinating. There's something romantic and exciting about all those goods sailing around the world. Silk from China. Spices from India. Cars from Germany."

Thor rolled his eyes.

"Our little port handles ninety million tons of cargo every year."

I widened my eyes and tightened my grip on his arm.

"We're the only deep-water port linked to six railroads."

"Six?" I managed to make the number sound like a scandalous act.

Lyman glanced at Thor, then bent and whispered in my ear, "I'd be happy to give you a private tour."

"I'd love that."

"When are you free?"

"Adele's keeping me very busy, but I'll make the time. For you."

"Poppy! There you are." Patrice Coombs removed my hand from Lyman's arm and held it. "Nice to see you, Lyman. Mark, we're so glad you're here. Now, Poppy. There are people who are simply dying to meet you. Lyman, may I steal her from you?" She didn't wait for a response. Instead, she pulled me away.

I offered Lyman, the man with information I wanted, a fleeting apologetic smile, and let myself be pulled.

When we were well away from the cabana, Patrice stopped pulling. "I don't want to interfere, dear, but stay away from that man. Pete does business with him, so we had to invite him, but he's not—" she searched the crowded party for the right word "—nice."

"Thank you for your concern, but he was just telling us about the port."

"The port? How dull."

"I found it fascinating."

"Really?"

I nodded.

"Then let me introduce you to my cousin Reynard. He knows all about the port."

When one door closed, another door opened. "I'd like that."

"You stay right here and I'll find him." Patrice disappeared into the crowd.

"What did that guy whisper in your ear?" Thor's brows were drawn in a thunderous expression.

"He offered to give me a private tour of the port."

"I bet he did."

"I might learn something."

"You think that guy knows anything about smuggling? Or drugs?" Thor's dark face lightened. "He's probably familiar with Viagra."

"He might know something."

Thor rolled his eyes. "There are better ways to get information about the port."

"Name one."

"Wikipedia."

"Name two."

"Patrice's cousin Reynard."

Well. If he was going to be smart about things.

A waiter passed by and I grabbed two fresh glasses of Champagne off his tray and handed one to Thor. "We're at a party. At least pretend you're having fun."

"That might be easier if you didn't flirt with every man here."

"I'm not really flirting."

"What's that's supposed to mean?"

"There's no intent." And Thor wasn't really my date. If he was, I'd be dancing, not tracking down information.

"You want me to have fun? Fine. Let's da—"

"This way, Poppy." Patrice reclaimed her hold on my arm and pulled me through the crowd.

With a scowl that reached all the way to his hairline, Thor followed.

"Reynard Coombs, meet Poppy Fields. Poppy, this is our cousin, Reynard."

Reynard smiled up at me. He possessed a shock of white hair and currant eyes that glittered past the wrinkles on his face. In his right hand, he held a silver-knobbed cane. His thumb moved across the silver—back and forth. He patted the floral cushion next to him on a wrought-iron settee. "Sit down, my dear. Patrice tells me you're interested in the port."

I sat. "I am."

Patrice took the admission as her cue to leave. "There are people I must talk to. Enjoy your evening."

Reynard sized me up with his glittering eyes.

I did the same. The man was ninety if he was a day.

"It seems Patrice has killed two birds with one stone."

"Pardon?"

"She's found someone to tell you about the port and someone to keep this old man company. Now, tell me, why are you interested in the port?"

I blinked.

"Of all the fabulous places in New Orleans, why the port?"

Thor, who'd taken the wrought-iron chair next to mine, cleared his throat. "She's interested in smuggling." Apparently he'd decided—without consulting me—on the direct approach.

"New Orleans has a long and glorious history of smuggling. Have you heard of Jean Lafitte?"

"No."

"Pirate. Smuggler. Hero." Reynard's thumb rubbed across the silver of his cane—faster now. "Do you know why the Port of New Orleans is important?"

I didn't. I shook my head.

Thor gave me a pitying look. "New Orleans is the access point to the Mississippi."

"Does that matter anymore?"

Reynard's eyes sparkled. "More than ever. It's the cheapest form of transportation available. There are trains of barges more than two thousand feet long that can be driven by as few as two towboats." Reynard leaned against the back of the settee and steepled his fingers. "Let's start at the very beginning."

Reynard happily told me why New Orleans was located at the bend in the river. Then he explained privateering and gave me a detailed description of the Battle of New Orleans. As far as I could tell, we were about two hundred years from the information I wanted. My gaze wandered across the patio.

I stiffened.

"What?" Thor's voice was low enough not to disturb Reynard's tale of a pirate's island called Campeche.

"Bad guy. Ten o'clock." The man from the Columns was here. Sipping a martini as if he belonged.

"Which one?"

"Dark hair. We should call the police." I touched Reynard's arm. "I'm sorry to interrupt your story, but—" I nodded toward man from the Columns and the man to whom he was speaking "—who are they? The man with the dark hair looks so familiar." If I had a name, I could tell Detective Langlois.

Reynard, who was recounting a tale of New Orleans during the Civil War, focused his gaze on the two men. He patted his suit pocket, took out a pair of glasses, and perched them on the end of his nose. He squinted. "I only know one of them. Quint Arnaut."

"Carter's father?"

"Carter's uncle."

"Knox's father?" I saw the resemblance now.

"You've met Knox?" Reynard shifted his glittering gaze to Thor. "Best keep an eye on Knox, Mr. Stone."

Knox Arnaut didn't stand a chance, and Thor wasn't really my date.

"You've never seen the other man?" I asked.

"Never."

It was at that moment that the two men, as if finally sensing they were the subject of intense scrutiny, looked at us.

Reynard waved.

Quint nodded—a curt I'm-deep-in-an-important conversation nod.

Reynard beckoned.

Perhaps there are places in the country where middle-aged men can ignore the summons of octogenarians. New Orleans was not one of those places. Quint said something to Columns man and headed our way.

Columns man looked at us—at me—as if trying to place us.

I donned my best I'm-so-pretty-I-don't-need-brains expression and his gaze moved on to Thor.

"Reynard. Nice to see you."

Reynard gazed up at Quint Arnaut and grinned. "Quint, I'd like to introduce you to Poppy Fields and her friend, Mark Stone."

"Poppy Fields? Adele's friend? I believe you had dinner with my son last night."

"I did. He took me to Antoine's." I smiled. "He looks just like you."

Arnaut turned to Mark and held out his hand. "Nice meeting you."

"Likewise."

"Reynard was just telling us the history of the Port of New Orleans."

"You won't find anyone in the whole city who knows more." Arnaut glanced over his shoulder. "If you'll excuse me, I'm talking business with—"

"It's a party, Quint. Save business for another time." The sugar in Reynard's voice had crystallized into something hard.

"Sadly, this deal won't wait." He took a step backward. "Poppy, Mark, nice meeting you. Reynard, always a pleasure." He took another step—a giant step—nodded, and returned to Columns man. The two walked away.

Reynard shifted his bright gaze my way. "You're not interested in the history of the port."

"Of course I am," I lied.

"With all due respect, Miss Fields, you're a terrible liar. What is it you want to know?

"I'd like to know what's being smuggled now."

"You should have asked Quint."

"Quint?"

"Quint Arnaut owns one of the largest shipping companies in the country. There's not much he doesn't know about moving cargo through the Port of New Orleans.

Chapter Eight

I slipped inside the Gearys' enormous house, found a quiet room—one filled with ferns and bamboo furniture and glass-topped tables—and called Detective Langlois.

"What do you want, Miss Fields?" The detective did not sound happy to hear from me.

"I spotted him again."

"Are you loitering on Dumaine?"

"No. I'm at an engagement party for Adele and Carter."

"Adele Coombs and Carter Arnaut? And you spotted the man who chased Vic Klein into the Columns?"

"Yes."

"He's at the party?" The disbelief in his voice bordered on insulting.

"Yes."

"Are you taking any medication I should know about, Miss Fields?"

I stood at the window with its view of the patio, tightened my free hand into a fist, and ground out, "No. Of course not."

On the patio, uniformed waiters were replenishing the

buffet—enormous grilled shrimp, raw oysters nestled on a bed of shaved ice, crab cakes, crawfish pies, beef tenderloin—the amount of food was overwhelming.

"You're sure you saw him?"

"Positive. He was talking to Quint Arnaut."

Detective Langlois answered with silence.

"I'm not making this up and I'm not on drugs." My annoyance shook its finger at his disbelief.

"What do you propose I do, Miss Fields? Disrupt your friend's party because you think you may have spotted a man you saw for five seconds?"

"It's him."

"Five stressful seconds."

I leaned my forehead against the glass. Detective Langlois didn't believe me. That, or he was unwilling to anger Pete Coombs by sending police to Adele's party.

"And when I get there, are you willing to tell Quint Arnaut that the man he's been chatting with is a killer?"

That would be an awkward conversation.

"This isn't your problem, Miss Fields. Let it go."

The man replenishing the crab cakes turned and my heart stuttered. The last time I'd seen him he'd been lying in the street. If I told Detective Langlois last night's mugger was at the party too, the detective might have me hauled in for a drug test —that or have me committed.

"Are you there, Miss Fields?"

"I'm here."

"Take my advice. Enjoy the party. Enjoy this time with your friend. Leave the bad guys to people who've been trained to handle them."

Detective Langlois would be no help. It was a good thing I had Thor. "Fine."

"Fine?"

"That's what I said. Fine." I had no intention of following Detective Langlois' advice, but I wasn't about to tell him that.

"Something tells me you're just placating me."

"Adele has me attending more parties than I can count. I'll leave chasing criminals to the people who've been trained." Keeping a sarcastic edge out of my voice took real effort.

"I'm holding you to that, Miss Fields. Enjoy your party." Detective Langlois hung up.

I stood at the window and watched the mugger put more oysters on ice.

What the hell was going on?

"What are you doing in here?"

I glanced over my shoulder at Thor. "I made a phone call."

"The police?"

I nodded.

"You left me with Reynard."

"Sorry."

"You don't look sorry."

"Well, I am."

"Would you like to dance?"

I stared at him while my tongue tied itself in complicated knots. Mute—that was me.

"I asked you to dance, not skinny-dip." Thor raised his brows. "You can dance?"

"Yes, I can dance." My first fourteen years were spent with my father—in Montana. I'd learned to ride horses and shoot guns and, thanks to the Krav Maga classes he insisted upon, protect myself. I spent my high school years with Chariss. Those years were more about dance classes and determining if I had enough talent for Hollywood. I didn't. But I could dance well enough to get by at a party.

Thor extended his hand.

I gazed at his fingers. "The guy Quint Arnaut was talking

to—he's the man who shot up the Columns. And the guy who tried to mug me—I just saw him replenishing the oysters."

"Someone tried to mug you?"

"Yes."

"And he's still walking around?"

"Obviously."

"You told the police?"

"I did—I called Detective Langlois. I told him about the guy from the Columns."

"And what did he say?"

"He'll handle it. I'm not to worry my pretty little head."

Thor's lips quirked. "You should let him."

"But—"

"Do you really want to spoil your friend's party?"

"Of course not."

"Then let it go. The police can get the man's name from Quint Arnaut. They can ask the caterer for the mugger's name."

What Thor was suggesting made sense. "But—"

"Dance with me."

Dancing with Thor would be...intimate. I hesitated.

"Please?" He led me outside, toward the dance floor. "You're the one who keeps telling me this is a party. So shut up and dance with me."

I had no argument for that.

Thor's hand on my waist was warm. My hand in his felt tiny.

And Thor could dance. Well. In his arms, I felt as if I were floating.

"The singer sounds just like Harry Connick, Jr."

I glanced at the band. "That is Harry Connick, Jr."

"You're kidding. They hired Harry Connick, Jr.?"

"More likely he's a guest and someone talked him into singing."

"Then I'm glad I chose this song to ask you to dance."

"What do you mean?"

He smiled down at me. "Shut up and don't ruin it for me."

I shut up. And Harry transitioned from "It Had to Be You" to "Let's Just Kiss."

Thor kept me in his arms.

And I didn't complain.

He spun me. The patio lights blurred into an enchanted kaleidoscope.

And, for an instant, I forgot about everything and everyone but the man who held me. My stomach fluttered. Fluttered. As if a herd of butterflies had invaded.

Nope. Couldn't do it. Could. Not. Do. It.

Thor and I had to work together. Neither butterflies nor the way my heart was beating too hard had any place in a professional relationship. Neither did this spinning sensation. I put as much space between us as Thor's hand on my lower back would allow. "We should go."

"It's Harry Connick, Jr."

"I didn't know you were a fan."

Thor's eyes searched my face and his lips thinned. He nodded. Once. As if I'd just confirmed his worst suspicion. "Where did you park the car?"

"Two blocks away."

After our extended lunch, Thor went for a walk, leading his shadow on a tour of French Quarter praline shops. While he sampled pecan candy, I drove one of James's cars to the Garden District and parked near the Gearys'.

The car waited for us.

Harry sang the last notes and we sidled off the dance floor.

"Do you have everything?"

"I need my evening bag." I nodded toward the small table where I'd left the clutch.

I picked up the little bag and we followed a garden path toward the back of the property—a couple sneaking off for a moment alone. At least that's what I hoped we looked like.

We followed the path into the shadows and stopped when we reached the fence—the eight-foot privacy fence.

"Can you get over that?" Thor cast a doubtful glance at my fitted dress.

I simply stared. The only way I was getting over that fence was if I hiked my skirt to my waist and Thor gave me a boost. "Maybe there's a gate."

"If there is, it'll be locked."

Thor was right. The Gearys would never allow unfettered access to the back of their property.

I kept staring—as if the weight of my gaze could shrink the damned boards to picket height.

Thor cleared his throat, a we-don't-have-all-night sound.

"I'll need your help."

"How do you want to do this?"

I looped the clutch's slender chain over my shoulder, kicked off my shoes, and hiked up my skirt. "You're going to have to boost me over. You can throw my shoes when I'm on the other side."

Better to focus on getting me over the fence rather than standing in front of Thor in a whisper of a thong.

"How—"

"If you'll cup your hands, I'll step into them. When you boost me, I'll throw my leg over the top."

"You're sure?"

Thor would be left on the ground looking at my ass as I hefted myself to the other side. Not ideal. I was open to suggestions. "Can you think of another way?"

Thor's gaze was fixed twelve inches above my head. "Let's do this." He crouched near the ground and closed his eyes.

I lifted a foot into his interlocked fingers.

And we froze.

Someone else was on the path.

They—a bleary-eyed couple—stopped when they saw us.

"Heh-heh," the guy chuckled.

"Sorry to interrupt." The woman winked at me.

There I stood, my skirt up, my foot in Thor's hands. And there was Thor, crouched—his face at eye-level with my whisper of a thong.

"It's not what it looks like."

"Too bad." The woman tittered and pulled on the man's arm, leading him farther down the path.

"They thought you were—" I couldn't say it.

"Let's get you over the fence." The blush on Thor's cheeks was visible in the darkness.

Or maybe that was my imagination. Possibly transference. My entire body was aflame with embarrassment. "Fine." The less said the better.

"On three?"

"Fine."

"One, two, three—" He boosted me upward.

I grabbed the top of the fence and swung a leg over.

I landed in soft grass on the other side.

"Are you okay?" he called softly.

"Fine." I yanked my dress into place. "Throw over my shoes."

One Jimmy Choo landed on the grass next to me, the other glanced off my shoulder.

"Are you coming?"

The fence groaned with Thor's weight.

A second later he was beside me. I couldn't look at him.

Could not. Which was ridiculous. Ridiculous but true. "Let's get out of here."

Keeping to the shadows, we snuck past a gazebo and large shrubs. We crouched behind a crepe myrtle when a light at the back of the house came on. I held my breath until it went off.

Thor tripped over a lawn wicket.

I tripped over a garden hose.

The Gearys' neighbor's backyard was a minefield.

Finally, we escaped, and I peeked at my phone to get my bearings.

"The car's that way." I pointed.

We walked a block in silence.

"Someday we'll laugh about that," Thor ventured.

No need to ask what *that* was. "Today is not that day."

"I tried not to look."

I peeked at him out of the corner of my eye. He wasn't smirking. Not that I could see. "Let's talk about something else."

"Like what?"

"This Mason Hubbard guy?"

"What about him?"

"He's a musician?"

"Yes."

"So, how does he know what's going on at the port?"

"Mr. Brown gave me his name."

"And that's all he gave you?" If—and it was a big if—Mr. Brown had ever been taught to share, the lesson hadn't extended as far as information. He guarded secrets like a dragon guarded its horde.

"That's all he gave me."

. . .

FIGURED. I nodded my chin toward the car parked at the curb. "There it is."

"That's a Portofino." Awe tinged his voice.

"Yes."

"A Ferrari Portofino."

As if I didn't know who manufactured Portofinos. "Does that mean you want to drive?"

Thor's hand closed around my elbow. "You left that car out here by itself?"

"The plan wouldn't have worked if I stayed with it."

"Poppy, that car costs a quarter of a million dollars."

"And it's insured." Men and cars. I didn't get it. In my opinion—not that James asked—Ferraris were terrible in-town cars. Yes, they were pretty. Yes, James's Ferrari was pretty and red. But they were built to drive fast—not an easy thing to do on New Orleans' congested streets.

Apparently, Thor didn't share my opinion. With a reverential expression on his face, he slid behind the wheel. He grinned when the engine growled to life.

I relaxed into the passenger seat.

Thor put the car in gear. "Wow."

"Go, Speed Racer, go."

He stretched his fingers, then tightened them around the wheel.

Thor drove. Fast. Of course.

In no time, we were on Esplanade. With a pained expression on his face, Thor parked James's car.

We paused on the banquette and, for a moment, I worried Thor wouldn't be able to leave the Ferrari.

Somehow he tore himself away and we walked through a few blocks of jasmine-scented air to Frenchmen Street.

"Which club?" I asked.

"The Tiger's Eye."

I searched the signs—a striped cat who looked vaguely like a demon blew on a sax. "There."

"Dammit."

"What?"

Thor jerked his chin at the people waiting to get in. "The line."

"Don't worry about it."

His eyes narrowed. "What are you going to do?"

"Be me." If being Poppy Fields didn't work, I'd slip the bouncer a hundred. One way or another, we were skipping that line and connecting with Mason Hubbard.

"Oh my God! Oh my God! You're Poppy Fields!" A girl with white blonde hair, a deep tan, and a stunned expression looked at me as if she couldn't believe I was standing a few feet from her. "Can I get a picture?"

She didn't wait for my response. She just whipped out a cell, leaned close to me, and smiled at her screen.

"What are you doing here?" Her voice was ridiculously high.

"Just here for some music."

"That's so cool. You're a Firebirds fan?"

I looked at Thor. Firebirds?

"I'm the fan," said Thor.

"I know Rocko."

"Rocko?"

"The bouncer. I can get us past the line. Come with me."

We followed her to the front of the line, where Rocko sat on a rickety stool with his arms crossed over the impossibly huge expanse of his black-tee-shirt-covered chest. The girl whispered in his ear.

Rocko took a moment to study Thor and me with world-weary eyes.

He nodded and we were in.

A band set up on a tiny stage at the front of the club. A woman in her thirties with roses tattooed across her chest rubbed her neck. A pale, gangly man with aviators perched on his nose fiddled with a saxophone. A middle-aged man with seventies sideburns and a newsboy cap stretched his fingers over a keyboard. A bald guy with a spare tire barely covered by a plaid shirt plucked at the strings of a double bass.

Our friend from the street led us to the bar.

"What can I get you?" Thor asked.

"Turbodog," she replied.

A what? "Do you come here often?" Duh. Obviously, she did. She knew Rocko.

She nodded. "It's my favorite place. Look—" she pointed "—there at the end of the bar." She dashed through a cluster of people and nabbed two stools.

Thor joined us and handed the girl a beer bottle with a yellow label. He handed me one too. "Turbodog."

"Thanks?"

"It's a local beer." He turned to the girl. "I'm Mark Stone."

"Sissy Palmer."

"Thanks for getting us in."

Sissy shrugged. "No problem.

"Which one is Mason Hubbard?" I nodded toward the stage—really just a platform in front of a large window with a mirror angled above.

"He's on the piano," Sissy replied.

The middle-aged guy.

Did Sissy know him? If so, what could she tell us?

The woman with the rose tattoos stepped up to the mic and the bar went quiet. The rasp in her voice conjured determination and hope and heartache. I closed my mouth and listened.

"She's good, right?" Sissy smiled at me as if she'd discovered the woman on stage.

I nodded.

"She always leads off with 'Angel from Montgomery.' Always. Her name is Rose O'Leary."

I could make a call and Rose would have record people beating down her door. I would make a call. Right after we talked to Mason Hubbard.

The song's last notes lingered in the humid air. When they faded, chords from Mason Hubbard's keyboard took their place.

I gazed at the mirror angled above the stage and watched his fingers fly.

Rose sang "Iko Iko," then a song I didn't know.

Thor leaned toward me as if he had something to say.

I lowered my ear.

Bang!

Glass shattered.

People screamed.

The music died.

Thor launched toward me, knocking me from my stool. My head thudded against the floor.

Bang! Bang! Bang!

Then nothing.

Thor was on top of me, his breath loud in my ear. Neither of us moved. We didn't trust the silence.

A second passed and Thor raised up onto his hands and knees. "Hell."

I followed the direction of his gaze.

Sissy Palmer stared sightlessly at the ceiling.

Thor reached into his jacket and pulled out a Glock. "Are you okay?"

There were two of everything. And, if I tilted my head, there were four. "Yeah."

He ran for the door. Both of him.

Near me someone screamed into a phone, "I'm at The Tiger's Eye. There's been a shooting. People are hurt."

I pushed myself off the floor and lurched toward the stage. The window looking out onto the street lay in shards on the floor. The saxophone player's glasses were gone and he looked at me with stunned eyes.

Rose huddled on the floor. Blood welled between the fingers she held clasped to her shoulder.

Mason Hubbard was gone.

Chapter Nine

I turned a slow circle and searched for the missing pianist.

That's when I saw her. The woman from the Séance Room. Mama Vielle.

She scuttled toward me and closed her gnarled hand around my elbow. "C'mon, we gotta go."

What? And why was the room spinning? "No. I can't leave." I couldn't abandon Sissy.

I planted my feet and watched Rose O'Leary struggle to hers. She and the saxophonist stumbled toward the front door.

Mama Vielle's lips thinned and she tugged on my arm. "We gotta get you outta here. Now. Before anything else happens."

"What else could happen?"

"Bad things."

Someone I didn't know—someone tall and dark who smelled of the night—took my other arm. And the two of them led toward the back of the destroyed club.

"Hurry, now." Mama Vielle pulled me past the bathrooms, through an emergency exit, and into a wide alley.

I gulped night air.

"C'mon." She wasn't done pulling. "We're still too close."

The world was off-kilter, tipping from side to side. I touched my scalp and found a large lump.

"There used to be an art market back here." Mama Vielle spoke gently as if I were a spooked animal. "But a developer bought that property—" she waved her hand at a building "—and closed down the market."

I glanced back. Somehow the bar was thirty feet behind us.

"I don't understand what's happening." My brain was fuzzy.

"Trust me."

"I don't know you."

"Papa Legba came to me in a dream and told me to get you outta there."

"Papa Legba? Who's Papa Legba?" And where was Thor? When he returned and found me gone, he'd be worried.

"Papa Legba helped get you outta that bar."

The man who took my other arm. What had happened to him? "Where is he now?"

"Papa Legba don't stick around. He's the gatekeeper between worlds. He's busy."

My brain was definitely fuzzy. "You mean a drug dealer?"

Mama Vielle snorted. "He's a loa."

"A what?" I looked over my shoulder. The Tiger's Eye was fifty feet behind us. "I should go back. My friend will be looking for me."

Mama Vielle tightened her hold. "We're not going back there."

"Why no—"

Kaboom!

A blast of air and sound knocked me to the ground.

Then came heat.

I opened my eyes and saw Mama Vielle sprawled on the pavement next to me.

Tiny pieces of grit bit into my palms and my knees. I sat. Slowly. Then I gaped at the source of the explosion.

Half of the Tiger's Eye was demolished. The other half was on fire. Anyone who'd remained inside—oh, God. Where was Thor? What if he'd come back for me?

I struggled to my feet, but the pavement shifted. Or at least that's what my head and stomach told me. I stumbled to the solid support of the nearest building, leaned against a wall, and vomited.

When nothing remained in my stomach, I spit and wiped my mouth with the back of my hand. "Are you all right?"

Mama Vielle hadn't moved and she didn't answer me.

I took a deep breath, tested the steadiness of the concrete beneath my feet, and lurched toward her.

"Mama Vielle, are you all right?"

She didn't stir.

I pressed my fingers against her wrist and found a pulse. Not dead. Not dead was good. We could work with not dead.

My little clutch lay on the ground a few feet from where I'd fallen. I grabbed the chain handle and pulled it to me.

The phone inside gleamed like the promise of salvation. I dialed 911.

"What's your emergency?"

I could barely hear the woman who'd answered my call. I stuck a finger in my free ear. "I was at the Tiger's Eye—"

"Help is on the way, ma'am."

"We exited the back before the explosion—"

"I have reports of a shooting, ma'am."

"The building blew up."

"Blew up? You mean exploded?"

"Exactly. I'm in the back alley and the woman I'm with isn't moving. Isn't responding."

"How long ago was the explosion, ma'am?"

"Maybe a minute."

"I'm dispatching additional cars and ambulances. Can you tell me what happened?"

Did the woman on the other end of the phone not understand what an explosion was? My voice rose a full octave. "The building blew up. What's left of the structure is on fire."

"What's your name, ma'am?"

"Poppy."

"Help is on the way, Poppy. I need you to stay calm."

Stay calm? What if Thor was in the building when it blew?

I glanced down at Mama Vielle. I couldn't leave her but—Thor. Flames hungrily devoured the bar's remaining walls. Heat from the fire warmed my cheeks. Anyone who'd been inside the Tiger's Eye when it exploded was beyond help.

My heart beat like a kettle drum. Where was Thor?

"Are you hurt, Poppy?" The 911 operator's calm tone promised all would be well.

"Me? No."

"Can you tell me exactly where you are?"

"I already did. We're in an alley behind the Tiger's Eye. Mama Vielle said there used to be an art market back here."

"Mama Vielle?" The cool professionalism in the woman's voice faltered.

"Yes. That's who's hurt."

"Older black woman?" Disbelief edged professionalism out of the way.

"Yes."

"Who are you?" Professionalism got miffed and left.

"Poppy Fields."

A few seconds ticked by. "How do you know Mama Vielle?"

"I met her at the Séance Room. She showed up tonight and told me Papa Legba sent her."

Now the voice on the other end of the line was faint. So faint I wasn't sure what the woman said.

I listened—hard—but sirens sliced through the night air, even louder that the roar of flames. "You'll have to speak up."

The operator mumbled her response.

A figure emerged at the end of the alley.

I squinted, but smoke and ash from the explosion made determining more than a vague shape impossible.

It was probably a police officer. Who else could it be?

The figure drew closer and my stomach tightened. Whoever he was, he wasn't with the police. There was something sinister about the way his shadow walked before him.

I shrank into the darkness. "There's someone coming toward us," I whispered into the phone. "And he's not friendly."

Papa Legba? No. The man who'd held my arm in the club had been tall and gangly. The man who walked toward me now was shorter.

"Police officers will be with you within a few minutes."

"Please, tell them to hurry."

Was that a gun in the man's hand?

I couldn't leave Mama Vielle. Not after she'd been hurt saving me. I scanned the alley, searching for a way to protect us. There were cigarette butts, fast-food wrappers, crushed soda cans, and a broken longneck bottle.

I picked up the bottle.

Not that a piece of glass would do much against a gun.

My mouth went dry.

"Are you there, Poppy?" I'd forgotten about the operator and her voice startled me.

"I'm here."

"The police are on scene."

They might be out front, but here, in the alley, I was on my own. "I don't see them." All I saw was the stranger and his gun.

If Detective Langlois hadn't taken my gun, I might have a chance.

"Stop there." Sounding authoritative when scared half to death wasn't easy.

Or effective. The man didn't stop.

"I mean it. Stop."

He raised his arm.

This was it. He'd use his gun while he was still far enough away to avoid the bottle's jagged edges.

"Stop!" I took a step toward him and blinked, nearly blinded by the sudden glare of red and blue lights.

The man lowered his arm and ran past me—a blur of smoke and shadow.

I still clutched the bottle. "Down here," I called to the police officer who got out of the patrol car. "We're down here and my friend needs an ambulance."

A patrol officer hurried down the length of the alley. "What happened?"

"The explosion knocked her down."

He fixed his gaze on the bottle in my hand.

"I picked it up when that man came toward us."

"What man?"

"The man. You must have seen him. Your arrival made him run away." Using the bottle, I pointed toward the other end of the alley.

"I didn't see anyone. You want to put that down please?"

I crouched and dropped the bottle onto the pavement.

The policeman bent and checked Mama Vielle's pulse. Then he spoke into the radio attached to the shoulder of his uniform. "We need an ambulance in the alley behind Tiger's Eye."

I leaned against the nearest wall and ignored the shivers in my knees and the fuzziness in my brain. "You're sure you didn't see anyone?"

"I didn't see anyone but you." His expression softened. "You've been through a lot. Trauma can make a person see funny things."

An argument rose to the tip of my tongue, but I sealed my lips. No good would come of arguing with the man trying to help us. Instead, I asked, "Will she be okay?"

He didn't answer.

"Can you make the ambulance come any faster?" If Mama Vielle hadn't forced me to leave, I'd have been in the club when it blew up. "She saved me."

His brows rose.

"She made me leave. If I hadn't—" My gaze returned to the burning building. Fire had consumed everything but the bricks.

An ambulance nosed around the corner and rolled toward us.

Where was Thor? Mark. Where was Mark? My throat tightened and I rubbed the bump on my head.

"Are you hurt?" asked the officer.

"I hit my head."

"We'll have them take a look at it." He nodded at the EMT who hurried toward Mama Vielle.

"I'm fine." The tears blurring my vision proved me a liar. "She's the one who needs help."

"You don't look fine."

"I was with a friend and I don't know what's happened to him."

"Can you call him?"

Duh. I pulled up Thor's—Mark's—contact information, pressed the button, and listened to the ringtone.

When voicemail picked up, I disconnected—I didn't trust my voice.

I glanced down at Mama Vielle. She hadn't moved since the explosion. At least now she was surrounded by EMTs—one checked her pulse, another attached one of those donut thingies around her neck, still another positioned a stretcher on the ground next to her.

I texted Mark. I made it out. Going to the hospital. Call or text when you can.

The EMTs shifted Mama Vielle to the stretcher and lifted her onto a gurney.

"This woman has a head injury." The police officer pointed at me.

One of the EMTs peeled away from the group loading Mama Vielle into the ambulance. "Where?"

I touched my head.

"May I?"

I nodded.

Gentle fingers explored the bump. "I'm going to look into your eyes, okay?"

"Okay."

He shined a penlight into my eyes.

I blinked.

"Headache or nausea?"

"Both," I admitted. "And I'm dizzy."

"Are you on any medications?"

"No."

"You need to be checked out."

No arguments. "May I ride with Mama Vielle?"

His gaze swung back to the ambulance. "That's Mama Vielle?" He whistled through his teeth. "C'mon."

"Wait," said the police officer. "I need your contact information."

"My name is Poppy Fields. Detective Langlois knows how to find me."

The short ride to the hospital took an eternity. At least that's how it seemed. I spent the whole trip alternating between checking my phone—no calls, no texts, no Mark—and staring at Mama Vielle. "Will she be okay?"

"We'll take good care of her."

No promises.

The ambulance pulled into a bay and two women in scrubs wheeled Mama Vielle away. A third forced me into a wheelchair.

The corridors were bright—power-of-a-thousand-suns bright—and I wished for sunglasses. Dark ones like the saxophone player wore.

Was he okay? Had Rose made it to safety? Where was Mark?

I endured an examination, countless questions, a diagnosis (a bump on the head), countless forms, and countless minutes of worry.

No calls, no texts, and the battery died.

Finally, a nurse told me I could leave.

"The woman I arrived with—Mama Vielle—how is she?"

"I'm sorry, I can't discuss other patients with you."

"Who can?"

"No one. Not without Ms. Winchester's permission."

"Ms. Winchester?"

"That's her real name—Ruby Winchester."

"You're sure no one will tell me anything?"

She nodded. "I'm sorry. We can't."

"Fine. My phone's dead. Could someone please call me a cab or an Uber?"

"Sure."

A taxi took me to Esplanade, where James's car waited at the curb. I'd half-hoped Mark would be with the car. He wasn't. The sinking sensation in my stomach left me gasping for air.

"You aren't gonna throw up, are you? It's extra if you throw up."

"No. I'm not going to throw up." I paid the fare, got out of the cab, and slid behind the wheel of the Ferrari.

I could search for Mark. But where? I had no idea and, according to doctor's orders, I wasn't supposed to drive or operate heavy machinery. I started the engine and sat, listening to the Italian machine growl like a hungry demon.

There was nothing so mundane as a phone charger in James's car, and the dark face of my cell told me finding power was more important than wandering New Orleans looking for Mark.

I drove home, pulled the Ferrari into James's coach house, and turned off the ignition.

In the silence that followed, I rested my head against the steering wheel.

If Mark wasn't here, what should I do? Call the police? Call Mr. Brown?

I wiped my eyes and swallowed the lump in my throat.

I was probably overreacting. Or not. Mark had chased after an unknown assailant—and not come back. What if he had come back? What if he'd been in The Tiger's Eye looking for me when the building blew to smithereens?

If he wasn't inside, I'd call Mr. Brown. I swung open the car door and lowered my left foot to the pavement.

"Where the hell have you been?"

He was alive. Scowling at me. Relief flooded my veins and I sagged into the seat. Alive. And barking at me.

"Well, where were you?" His brows were drawn, his arms were crossed, and he looked ready to spit nails.

He was angry? With me? He was the one who hadn't returned my text. "I was at the hospital. Why didn't you get back to me?"

"The hospital?" His eyes scanned my body as if he expected to see a cast or a missing limb. "What happened?"

He'd tackled me and my head had connected with the floor.

"Long story." I scanned him too—he was the type to dismiss a stab wound as a minor cut. "Why didn't you answer? I was worried."

"You were worried?" Righteous indignation puffed his cheeks and straightened his spine. "*You* were worried?"

"Yes. I was worried. You chased after a gunman and didn't return my text."

"I left you alone for ten minutes and a building blew up."

"I can hardly be blamed for that." I swung my right foot onto the pavement and stood. "Why didn't you return my text?" He'd better have a damned good reason for putting me through hell.

His face flushed. "I broke my phone. But you—" he fisted his hands "—you've been ignoring your calls. When I got back here, the first thing I did was call you. You didn't answer."

"Battery is dead." I shook the lifeless cell at him. Being angry was the easy emotion. Far easier to rage than admit how much I cared when I thought something awful had happened to him.

He narrowed his eyes. "I thought you were gone."

"Gone?"

"Dead."

"I'm not. And I could say the same."

He closed the distance between us and circled my upper arms with his hands. "I've been losing my mind."

"Me too." I glared up at him.

Something electric sparked between us.

His grip on my arms tightened. "You could have checked in with Ladybug."

"I—" My voice faltered. He was right. If I'd called Ladybug, neither of us would have had to worry. But I wasn't used to having anyone at home. Well, no one but Consuela. And as amazing as she was, she couldn't yet relay phone messages. "I didn't think."

"You didn't think." He loosened his hold on me and took a step backward.

"It's not as if I was out having fun. I was at the hospital."

"Why?"

"The woman who got me out of the building was knocked out by the explosion."

"So you're not even hurt?"

"You sound disappointed. For your information, I hit my head. Hard."

He pointed at the Ferrari. "And you drove?"

Thor was an idiot. "Yes, I drove."

"You left the hospital and got a ride to the car instead of coming home?"

"I thought you might be with the car."

"Why would I be with the car?

"Because you seemed worried when we left it on Esplanade."

"*Yip*!" Consuela had escaped the confines of the house and she did not approve of our argument.

I bent, held out my arms to her, and—swayed. Steadying myself with my right hand on James's car, I stood. Slowly.

"What's wrong?" Thor demanded.

"I told you. I hit my head. Would you please pick Consuela up for me?"

He scooped her into his arms, then deposited her in mine. "How did you get hurt?"

"You knocked me off a bar stool."

His cheeks paled.

I snuggled Consuela against my chest.

"I hurt you?" His voice was raw.

"It was an accident."

"*Yip.*" Shame on him.

I kissed the silky top of Consuela's head. "An accident, and I'll be fine. I'm glad you're not hurt or dead or—" I took a deep breath. "If you don't mind, I'm going to bed." I walked past him.

"Poppy—" He stopped me with a hand on my arm.

I looked up into his face. Pain and worry and regret and an emotion I wouldn't name stormed in his eyes. My poor abused heart stuttered. "Let's talk in the morning when we're not so—"

He released me. Slowly. Then he rubbed his eyes. "Yeah. Fine."

Looking straight ahead, I entered the house.

"*Yip, yip.*" Consuela knew what was what. Thor and I were a pair of idiots.

Chapter Ten

Detective Langlois arrived at James's house early on Saturday morning. The detective's eyelids drooped and the bad-boy smirk I'd noticed on Thursday was gone. In its place, his lips formed a thin, humorless line.

I took pity on him. "May I offer you some coffee?"

His eyes narrowed as if being offered coffee was a rare occurrence.

"You look as if you might need some."

He rubbed the back of his neck. "This isn't a social call."

"I didn't imagine it was. But you look like you need coffee." And a shower. And twelve hours of sleep.

I turned to Ladybug, who lingered in the front hallway after letting him in. "May we have coffee in the living room, please?"

"Yes, ma'am."

I led Detective Langlois into the living room and perched on a club chair.

Detective Langlois settled on the couch across from me. When the sound of Ladybug's steps receded down the hall, he crossed his ankle over his knee and leaned back, a considering look on his face. "What happened to you last night?"

"Someone shot up the Tiger's Eye and blew up the building."

"I know that. I want to know what you were doing at The Tiger's Eye." His tone said I'd better not continue stating the obvious.

"Listening to music." No need to mention Mason Hubbard. "There was an amazing singer. I think her name is Rose O'Leary. And a phenomenal pianist. Did they make it out okay?"

The skin near Detective Langlois' left eye twitched. "When I spoke with you, you were at a party in the Garden District." Apparently he wasn't offering updates on the band members' welfare.

"I was."

"How did you get to Frenchmen Street?"

"We drove."

The hand resting on the back of the couch clenched into a fist. "We?"

"Me and Mark Stone."

Twitch, twitch, twitch went the skin near his eye. "Who is Mark Stone?"

"A friend."

Detective Langlois looked down at the floor. His shoulders lifted as if he were taking a deep, cleansing breath. "Why did you go to Frenchmen Street?"

"I already told you, we went to listen to music."

"When did you arrive in New Orleans, Miss Fields?"

"Thursday morning."

He nodded as if I'd confirmed his worst suspicions. "Since then, there's been a massive shooting on St. Charles Avenue, a shooting on Frenchmen Street, and a building has been reduced to rubble. People are dead."

"Are you suggesting I was involved in any of those things?"

Twitch, twitch, twitch. "If the shoe fits."

Oh, please—that was ridiculous. And troubling. "I told you everything. I described the man I saw at the Columns." My voice rose slightly. "I called you when I spotted him on Thursday night. When I saw him last night, I called you again."

Detective Langlois lifted his gaze and scowled at me. "What happened at The Tiger's Eye?"

I would not be put off by his question. "Why haven't you done anything about the man I saw? Why haven't you arrested him? At least brought him in for questioning? Quint Arnaut knows his name."

Detective Langlois rested his arms on the back of the couch as if he were relaxed. I wasn't fooled—his eye twitched like mad. "I'll ask the questions."

"Maybe you should direct your questions to someone who can answer them. Like that man. I don't know anything." Not exactly true, but Detective Langlois's refusal to go after the man I'd seen made me wonder about him. Just as I wondered about Quint Arnaut. And Knox. I didn't trust any of them.

We glared at each other.

The detective looked away first. "What do you know about conducting an investigation?"

Only what I'd seen on the movies and television. "I know when someone identifies a man involved in a high-speed chase followed by a murder the police should pick the guy up. Ask a question or two."

He shifted his gaze to the paintings on the wall.

"It's almost as if you don't want to talk to him."

"There are things you don't know, Miss Fields."

"Everything okay in here?" Thor stood in the doorway—

lounged in the doorway. He wore faded jeans and an untucked button-down shirt. His feet were bare. His hair was tussled. His body language, voice, and expression matched his appearance. Laid back. So why did I have the impression throttling Detective Langlois was high on his to-do list?

"The detective was just asking me about what happened last night."

Thor's brows rose. "Oh?"

A few seconds passed.

Thor rolled his neck. "Aren't you going to tell him?"

I shot him the death glare he deserved. "I already did. We were in the Tiger's Eye when someone shot through the front window. People panicked. They ran."

"And then?" asked Detective Langlois.

"The building blew up."

Twitch, twitch, twitch. "How did you get out?"

"The back door."

"Alone?"

"No."

"With Mr. Stone?" Detective Langlois jerked his chin toward Mark, who still leaned against the doorframe.

"No."

"With whom?" Detective Langlois already knew the answers to the questions. I was sure of it.

"Mama Vielle."

"And what did you do, Mr. Stone?"

"I ran out the front door."

"I'd think you'd want to stay with Miss Fields."

"Poppy is good at taking care of herself." Thor's gaze met mine. "Sometimes I forget just how capable she is."

Detective Langlois's eye twitched with manic energy. "We have reports of a man chasing the shooter away from the scene. I don't suppose you saw anyone doing that?"

Thor shook his head and smiled—a sunny, open, casual smile that said he didn't have a sneaky bone in his body. "Nope."

"How long are you in New Orleans, Mr. Stone?"

"I'm Poppy's date to her friend's wedding. As long as she's here, I'm here." His gaze shifted to the hallway. "Let me help you with that." He disappeared, reappearing a few seconds later carrying a tray.

Thor sauntered into the living room and put the tray on the table in front of me.

"How do you take your coffee, Detective?"

"Milk and sugar."

I poured him a cup.

"You went to the hospital with Mama Vielle?" He was still asking me questions to which he knew the answers.

"Yes."

"You told the social worker at the hospital you'd pay any of her bills not covered by insurance?"

So much for hospital privacy. I said nothing—just nodded.

"That was very generous of you."

I shrugged. "Mark, would you like coffee?"

"No, thanks."

"Have you known her long?" asked the detective.

"Mama Vielle? No."

"Then why did you offer to pay her bills? A hospital isn't a Starbuck's drive-thru line. People don't pay for other people's orders."

"It seemed like the right thing to do."

Detective Langlois stared at me, waiting for me to say more.

He'd be waiting a long time.

I poured myself a cup of coffee and lifted the cup to my lips.

"You have to admit, disaster seems to follow you, Miss Fields."

"Do you really think Poppy is involved in your crime wave?" Thor no longer sounded casual—he sounded dangerous.

"I think she's one of those women who attracts trouble. I don't want to see her killed. Pete Coombs wouldn't like it." The detective stood. He'd finished with us—for now.

I rose from my chair. It was a good thing Detective Langlois was leaving—I could barely hold my tongue.

Thump.

As one, our gazes shifted toward the built-in bookshelves. A single book lay on the floor.

"That was odd," said Thor.

"It's the ghost." I was only half-joking. If the ghost planned on tossing objects around, I'd need something stronger than Ladybug's chicory coffee in my cup.

"The ghost?" Thor's grin said he wasn't a believer. He strode across the room. "What does the ghost want us to read?" He bent, picked up the book, and read the title. *Trust No One.*

Detective Langlois shrugged as if having a ghost in the house was no big deal. "Your ghost is a cynic."

My ghost? *My ghost*? The ghost needed to haunt a different house. The ghost was giving me the heebie-jeebies. I reached for my coffee—the tremor in my hand was hardly noticeable. "A cynic? You think?"

The detective's gaze lit on my shaking fingers and his answering smile was so sharp, a careless woman could cut herself on its edges. "Definitely. If you can't trust the police, who can you trust?"

Thor returned the book to its shelf.

Detective Langlois walked toward the door to the hall.

"You're sure you don't know anything that could help me catch the shooter or the bomber?"

My mouth dropped open and I returned the cup to its saucer with a loud *clink*. "You don't think they're the same?"

"I don't. Generally speaking, when there's a shooting followed by a bombing, the shooting is bait to draw in emergency personnel. But that's not what happened."

Something like respect flickered in Thor's eyes. "If the shooter hadn't opened up, there would have been a lot more people in the bar when the building blew." Thor rubbed his chin. "The shooting cleared the building. But if the bomber wanted an empty building, he could have waited till the bar closed."

Detective Langlois nodded his agreement.

My gaze traveled between the two of them. "Do you really think there are two bad guys? A shooter and a bomber?"

Thor nodded. "Looks that way."

"So the shooter wanted someone dead? The bomber wanted to destroy the bar?"

That idea was almost as chilling as having a resident ghost.

There was a third possibility. A killer wanted to make absolutely certain his target was dead.

Detective Langlois stepped into the hall. "Please, Miss Fields, stay out of trouble."

"I'll do my best."

When the door to the street closed on Detective Langlois, Thor's eyes narrowed. "Geez."

"What?"

"That cop—using an investigation to get close to you."

"I don't think that's what he was doing."

"Don't be naïve. Of course he was. Are you ready to look for Mason Hubbard?"

"We can't."

"What do you mean we can't?"

"We're due at Audubon Park in an hour."

He blinked. "Why?"

"The picnic."

Thor opened his mouth, but no words came out. Instead he stared at me. Gaped.

"It's casual."

"Poppy, finding Mason Hubbard and those shipping containers is a priority."

"I know. But I didn't come here to track down drugs. I came to be in my friend's wedding. We can look for Mason Hubbard later this afternoon. Or I can go to the picnic by myself."

"Not happening."

"Then we're both going. And we both need to get changed."

Thor pursed his lips and sighed. "I have to buy a new phone."

"You're not getting out of this." Adele's mother had gone to a lot of trouble getting Thor added to the guest counts. His being a no-show wasn't an option.

He saw defeat staring him in the face. "What do I wear?"

"Khakis."

An hour later, Thor (the proud owner of a new phone) and I hopped off the streetcar across from Tulane. I glanced over my shoulder. "Is anyone following us?"

"That guy with the baseball cap. Maybe."

"But he stayed on the streetcar."

"Which stops every block or so. He could get off at the next stop and hurry back."

"Let's go then." I tugged his arm and we crossed St. Charles and entered the park.

Spanish moss draped the sprawling branches of live oaks. The occasional palm tree rustled its fronds. Birds tweeted.

Young children chased each other while their mothers watched from park benches. I took Consuela out of my oversized handbag (I'd smuggled her onto the streetcar) and placed her on the path.

She shook herself, then pointed her little nose in the air, taking in all the sniffs.

"Would you hold onto her?" I handed Thor the slender length of pink leather. "I want to pull up the map on my cell."

"*Yip.*" Consuela pulled on the leash. She was sure she knew the way. How could I doubt her?

I looked at the map anyway. "We need to go left."

"Where exactly are we going?"

"Newman Bandstand." I took a final look at the map, then reclaimed Consuela's leash.

She trotted down the path. I followed.

To our right stretched a lagoon. According to the map, a golf course lay on the other side of the water.

"I can't believe you brought that dog."

Consuela stopped in her tracks and showed Thor her teeth.

"Adele asked the hostess and she said it was fine."

"What's the point of this party?"

I tugged gently on Consuela's leash. "It's a shower for Adele and Carter."

"A shower?"

"Yes."

"What did you get them?"

"Today was easy. The hosts asked for a check for a group gift."

"What's the group gift?"

"Patio furniture."

Thor blinked. "Do you have to give a gift at each shower?"

"Yes."

"And buy a wedding gift?"

"Of course."

"What are you giving them?"

"I sent a cut-crystal ice bucket, matching glasses, and engraved ice tongs."

He made no comment.

"I wanted to give them something they'd actually use."

"So you went with an ice bucket?"

"Have you seen how much people in New Orleans drink?"

Rather than answer, he pointed to an island in the lagoon where a tree held so many snowy egrets in its branches it looked like Minnesota in a blizzard.

I pulled out my cellphone and took a picture.

"*Yip.*"

Since Consuela had adopted me, I'd become one of those women who took endless pictures of her dog. Although, in my case, it was because she was the cutest dog ever. And the most territorial—she didn't appreciate my taking photos of other animals.

"*Yip.*" *The birds need to fly away. Now.*

"They're bigger than you are," I warned.

"*Yip, yip.*" *She could take them.*

I snapped a photo of her snarling face and dropped my phone back in my handbag.

We strolled for ten minutes until we saw the bandstand. The stone structure was round. Two enormous plinths held a roof that looked like a flying saucer. A brick terrace reached for the lagoon's edge.

Tables were set with yellow gingham linens and enormous bowls of daisies. Lacy white umbrellas offered shade. A small crowd sipped drinks and admired the views (lagoon and oak alley).

Adele welcomed me with a hug. She reached up on her tiptoes and kissed Thor's cheek. "I'm so glad you're here."

"It's a great spot for a picnic. So pretty."

Adele nodded her agreement and I noticed her eyes looked glassy. She'd been drinking. "Mark, would you get us a couple of Champagne cocktails, please?" She nodded toward a bar.

"Of course."

We both watched him walk away.

"What's wrong?" I asked.

Adele's answering smile wasn't quite genuine. "Nothing. I saw you two dancing last night."

"The music was amazing. I mean—Harry Connick, Jr."

"Then I didn't see you again. Did you go home early?" Her brows rose. She thought we'd gone home to—

"I should have found you before we left. I'm sorry."

"If I were in your shoes, I'd go home early too. Where did you find him?"

Maybe if I hadn't been shot at, haunted, and nearly blown up, I would have anticipated Adele's question. Thor's reappearance, and the handing over of drinks, saved me from answering.

Adele smiled up at Thor. "I was just asking Poppy how you two met."

I choked on my Champagne cocktail.

Thor draped his free arm around my shoulders. "We met in Paris."

"You haven't been together long." Adele used a that-explains-why-you-left-early tone. Obviously we'd left her party because we couldn't keep our hands off each other.

"It feels like forever," said Thor.

I choked again.

His chiseled cheeks flushed. "I mean it feels as if I've known Poppy forever. I can't imagine not being near her."

Romantic or creepy stalker? Thor walked a fine line.

Adele smiled. Clearly she'd decided upon romantic. "How did you actually meet?"

Thor blinked. Telling her he'd been my agency-assigned bodyguard wasn't a possibility.

"Mark saved me from a horde of paparazzi." That had the benefit of being almost true.

Thor nodded. "Then we sat at the Hemingway Bar and talked for hours."

"Carter and I don't have a meet-cute."

Panic flashed across Thor's face. What was a meet-cute? "Oh?"

"We really have known each other forever."

"All that means is you know each other well enough to know Carter is the one."

Adele smiled at me. "Knowing everything isn't always everything it's cracked up to be. There's no mystery left."

"You must have at least one secret." Was Thor teasing her? "Poppy's got a million."

I scowled at him. "Have I told you about how my last boyfriend ended up dead in bed?"

"I'll take my chances."

"See? That's what I'm talking about? You guys have secrets and secrets add—" she searched for a word "—spice."

"You have one," Thor insisted. "You must."

"Not one."

"What about Carter?" I waggled my brows. "He has secrets."

"Carter?" Her voice was frankly disbelieving.

"We met Lamar Prentiss last night and he hinted that Carter has a deep dark secret."

"A deep dark secret?" Adele laughed. "Carter?"

"Everyone has secrets," said Thor.

"Not Carter." She beckoned to her fiancé. When he arrived at her side, she asked. "What is this deep dark secret I'm just now hearing about?"

"Secret?"

"Lamar has been dropping hints," I explained.

Carter paled—three shades closer to wan—and hesitated for four seconds too long. "I don't have any secrets."

"What did you do?" Adele's glassy stare took his measure. "I know! Is it when you got caught running naked through McGeehee our senior year?"

Now, in addition to looking pale, Carter looked embarrassed. "No. Let's drop it, Adele."

"I want to know. What's this big secret?"

The man passed from pale to ghostly white. Whatever his secret, he'd done something much worse than dangle his junk on the run.

I took pity on him. "What's McGeehee?"

"A girls' school," said Adele. "Streaking through campus used to be a rite of passage."

Definitely not a secret to turn white over. Running through McGeehee sounded like something men laughed about at high-school reunions, not something to make a man look nauseated—and Carter definitely looked as if he wanted to hurl. He swallowed. Audibly. "I never realized you knew I got caught at McGeehee."

Adele rolled her eyes. "I've known about that for years."

"You have?"

"I recognized you."

"We wore masks."

"It wasn't your face I recognized. You've got that—"

More information than I wanted. "It looks as if people are taking their seats. What are we having for lunch? I'm starved."

Adele glanced at the colorful tables. "Barbeque." Then she shifted her gaze to Thor. "Come with me, I'll show you where you're sitting."

Carter and I watched them walk away.

"Carter, I'm sorry. I asked Lamar Prentiss how he knew you and he said something about a youthful indiscretion. I didn't mean to cause a problem."

"It's not your fault." Carter's skin was still green-hued.

"Be that as it may, I'm sorry." Even as I said the words, I couldn't help but wonder what kind of trouble lurked in Carter's past.

Chapter Eleven

I followed Carter to one of the gingham-covered tables. Thor and I were seated with Patrice and Pete Coombs, Quint Arnaut, and a handful of people I hadn't yet met.

The wheels in my mind turned.

Rather than take the open chair next to Thor, I chose a seat next to Quint.

Thor's brows rose, but he said nothing.

Quint's brows also rose, but he pulled out my chair. "This is my lucky day."

I sat and smiled up at him. "I think it's mine."

Consuela sank onto her haunches. "*Grrr*." She didn't agree with my assessment. At all.

He sat.

I worried for his ankles—when Consuela took against someone, she didn't believe in half-measures.

I scooped her into my lap.

Quint ignored the little dog in my lap and leaned close to my ear. "Trouble in paradise?"

I glanced at Thor, who sat next to Patrice. "No, but I can talk to Mark whenever I want. It's a treat to talk to you."

Quint's answering smile didn't touch his eyes. "Did you have fun last night?"

"We did. It's not every day Harry Connick, Jr. sings at a party."

"Given who your mother is, I assumed you'd find New Orleans a bit dull."

"Not in the least. There are so many interesting people to talk to."

"If by interesting you mean slightly crazy, I have to agree."

"I wouldn't go that far." How to bring up the man he'd been talking to at the party?

"I noticed Patrice palmed you off on Reynard last night. You got both crazy and dull."

"Reynard was entirely charming." And a tad crazy. And more than a tad dull.

"You are a very polite young lady."

It was now or never. I fluttered my eyelashes and served up one of Chariss's best smiles. "I noticed you speaking to someone who looked familiar to me."

"Last night?"

"Yes," I purred. "Six feet tall, dark hair, brown eyes, a divot in his chin." I touched the center of my chin.

Quint's eyes narrowed.

"He wore a lime necktie."

He nodded. Once. "John Howard."

"Why would I recognize him? Is he on television?"

"No." Quint lifted a goblet filled with iced tea to his lips.

"The movies?" I knew that wasn't true. "Is he from New Orleans?"

"He lives here now."

"I wonder how I know him..." I paused, hoping he'd fill the silence.

"Maybe he's got one of those faces."

"Those faces?"

"People think they recognize him when they don't."

"Maybe..." I drew the word out and doubt rounded its edges. "How do you know Mr. Howard?"

"You're very curious." His tone was polite, but annoyance flashed across his face.

I'd stop with the questions when Quint told me what I wanted to know. "Am I?"

"You are." He smiled past me at a man taking the chair on the other side of me. "Have you met Brooks Avery? Brooks, this is Poppy Fields."

I looked up at a man who carried his extra weight with aplomb. Laugh lines radiated from the tanned skin near his eyes and the grin that stretched his face had me smiling too.

"Poppy, it's a pleasure. I'm a great fan of your mother's." He held out his hand.

My smile faltered a tiny bit. "Nice to meet you, Brooks."

His hand swallowed mine and he shook it hard enough to reverberate in my shoulder—hard enough to unsettle Consuela.

He settled into his chair. "How in the world is this seat still open?"

"I guess because no one has claimed it yet."

"How fortunate for me."

I glanced at Quint, but he'd turned his shoulder to me and was deep in conversation with Patrice.

"How are you finding New Orleans?" Brooks asked.

"Delicious. I'm afraid I'll need to go on a diet when I get home." Chances were good whatever training Mr. Brown had waiting for me would burn off every single calorie. At least I hoped so.

"We do know how to eat well."

I glanced again at Quint.

He was still ignoring me.

I stroked the top of Consuela's head. "How do you know Adele and Carter?"

"Carter's daddy, Bill, and I have been friends since we could walk."

"Bill? I thought Carter's father's name was Buzz."

"That's his nickname. His given name is William Taylor Arnaut." Brooks leaned back in his chair. "I hear you and Adele met at that school in California."

"We did. We were freshman roommates."

"Her momma worried about sending her so far away."

"I couldn't have asked for a better roommate or friend." I searched the patio until I spotted Adele at another table. She held a glass of wine to her lips. "And she and Carter seem perfect together."

"They are. They are."

"You watched Carter grow up?"

"I did."

"We were just talking about Carter's deep dark secret. Which, according to Adele, might or might not be running naked through the McGeehee School campus." I kept my tone light. "Do you know what his secret is?"

The lines at the edges of Brooks' eyes hardened. "I reckon if Carter has a secret, it's up to him to tell it."

"I suppose you're right." Given Brooks' expression, it was time to change the subject. "What should I see while I'm in New Orleans?"

"Do you like parades?"

I nodded.

"Then you should go down to the port. There's a warehouse filled with floats. Mardi Gras World."

A waiter appeared at our table. "The buffet is open and you're invited to the line." He waved toward a long table heaped with food.

Brooks stood and helped me out of my chair.

The buffet table was loaded with pulled pork, ribs, barbequed shrimp, potato salad, slaw, macaroni and cheese, fried okra, bourbon baked beans, and cornbread muffins.

"Now that looks good," said Brooks as he took a plate from the stack at the end of the table.

"A diet is definitely in my future."

Brooks chuckled and added a half-rack of ribs to his plate.

My own plate held a multitude of shrimp and a spoonful of slaw and some fresh cut tomatoes. I'd learned enough about New Orleans cooking to know saving room for dessert was important.

"Is that all you're eating?" asked Thor. He stood behind me in the line.

"Yes." I cut my eyes away from the line. "I have something to tell you."

"Oh?" His eyes scanned my face and his brows furrowed. "Later."

"Later?" We needed to call Mr. Brown as soon as possible. He'd get us all the information in the world about John Howard.

Thor bent and brushed his lips across my ear. "We're at a party," he whispered.

He was right. But I'd be calling Mr. Brown at the first opportunity.

We walked back to the table with our plates and I sat down between Quint and Brooks.

"Quint was just telling me you were at the Columns with Adele when it was shot up."

I nodded. "I was."

"That must have been terrifying."

"It happened too fast to be scared. There was an accident on St. Charles, then a man came running up the stairs to the veranda. He dashed inside and more men arrived. They're the ones who opened fire."

"Did you see any of the shooters?" Quint's voice was sharp.

I glanced at him. His face reflected a mild interest at odds with his tone.

"No," I replied. "I kept my head down. Why do you ask?"

"I'd hate for a girl like you to get drawn into the dirty underside of New Orleans."

Was Quint Arnaut threatening me? I forced a smile. "I would hate that too. The people who chased Vic Klein onto that veranda are killers."

Brooks looked up from his ribs. "From what I've read in the paper, it was only a matter of time till Vic Klein got himself killed."

Since I'd been the one to actually kill Vic Klein, I refrained from comment.

"There you go, Poppy." Quint's voice was like a pat on my hand—or my head. "Vic Klein deserved what he got."

"What about the other people on that veranda? One dead, one in critical condition. They didn't deserve to be shot."

"Things in New Orleans aren't always black and white," Quint replied.

If murder wasn't black, I shuddered to think what was.

AFTER A LONG LUNCH, a Zydeco band, and tasting my first Hurricane, Thor, Consuela, and I walked toward St. Charles.

The park was still full of people, but I took my phone from my handbag.

"Who are you calling?" asked Thor.

"Mr. Brown."

"Now?"

"I got a name for the man I recognized last night. The one who was at the Columns."

Thor glanced around us. "You should wait."

"But—"

"I'll call him."

Thor's offer made me pause with my finger above the screen. Mr. Brown spent a fair amount of time exasperated with me. A request from Thor might carry more weight. "You'd do that?"

"For you?" He nodded.

Consuela, who trotted next to us, rolled her eyes.

I glanced behind us. The path was near empty. If Thor's shadow was following, he or she was being particularly sneaky. "As soon as we get home?"

"The moment we walk through the door."

I hid Consuela in my handbag and we climbed onto the streetcar and settled onto a mahogany bench near the back. Afternoon sun glinted on the car's brass fittings and, above us, bare lightbulbs awaited darkness. "It feels as if we've stepped back in time."

Thor didn't reply.

Our legs touched and our shoulders brushed on the short bench (whoever first designed streetcars didn't take men of Thor's size into account). Not noticing the zing of electricity passing where we touched took most of my focus.

I needed a distraction. "Where should we start looking for Mason Hubbard?"

"I'll ask Mr. Brown when I talk to him." Thor kept his gaze locked on the passing street—large houses surrounded by iron fences, people strolling the banquette, and—

I poked him. "There's the Columns."

He turned his head and his eyes narrowed. "You were sitting out there?" He pointed to the veranda.

"Yep."

"You're lucky to be alive."

I didn't argue.

We rode the streetcar to Canal Street, then walked past cut-rate liquor stores, stores selling tee-shirts, voodoo dolls, strands of gold, green, and purple beads, and shot glasses, a fried chicken stand, a praline shop, a payday loan office, an outdoor café, and an adult video store. Turning onto Royal Street with its art galleries and antique stores was a relief.

When we reached James's house, I dug my keys out of my handbag and let us in.

Thor headed toward his room. "I'll call Mr. Brown."

He didn't want me listening. "Okay."

I followed Consuela to the kitchen.

"How was your picnic?" asked Ladybug.

"Fine. Thank you." Half my brain had followed Thor.

"Can I get you something?"

"Iced tea. And information."

"Information?"

"This is going to sound crazy, but is this house haunted?"

"Yes." Ladybug picked up a pitcher and poured the contents over ice. "Mint or lemon?"

"Lemon, please. Haunted by whom?"

"I don't rightly know. I just know there's a ghost. Has it been bothering you?"

"A bit."

"I can send for someone to burn some sage. The ghost won't go away, but sage does seem to calm it."

"There's someone who does that for a living?"

"Under normal circumstances, I'd call Mama Vielle, but

seeing as she's in the hospital. Maybe when she gets out. I hear she owes you a favor."

"It's the other way around. Mama Vielle got me out of the Tiger's Eye before the building blew up." Guilt poked at me. "I need to go see her. Which florist should I call about sending flowers?"

"I don't understand why you left a fancy party to go to that bar." Ladybug shook her head as if leaving a party in the Garden District for a club on Frenchmen Street was beyond her comprehension.

"Mark wanted to hear the band."

"Who was playing?"

"The Firebirds."

Ladybug stumbled and she laid her hands across her heart. "You're sure about that?"

"Positive. Do you know them?"

"I know the singer."

"Rose? I saw her and the saxophonist leave by the front door before the explosion. I'm sure she's fine."

"I need to call."

"When you do—"

"Yes?"

"Would you please ask if the pianist made it out okay?"

Her brows rose.

"He was very good."

"He is. I've heard him play." She rubbed her forehead with the flat of her palm. "I can't remember his name."

"Someone at the bar said his name was Mason. Mason Hubbard."

"That sounds right." She reached for the phone. "I'll ask after him."

"How do you know Rose?"

"I've known her since she was born. Her mother and I have

been friends since elementary school." Her hand closed around the receiver, but she paused. "Can I get you anything else?"

The woman wanted privacy. "No. Thank you."

I left her. Feeling at loose ends, I wandered back to the living room and considered Ladybug's suggestion. Would having the room saged calm the ghost? "Are you there?"

Consuela cocked her head and looked at me as if I'd lost my mind.

"That book didn't fall by itself," I told her.

"*Yip*." Well, duh.

I walked over to the bookcase and gazed at the titles. Whatever had made that particular book fall, it was back in its place now. I ran my finger down its spine and made a mental list. I needed to visit Mama Vielle, find Mason Hubbard, figure out how John Howard played into all this, call Lyman Cox—that I could do immediately.

I turned and reached for my handbag.

Thump.

On the floor lay a book.

I bent and picked up *Three Cups of Deceit*.

"Who's deceitful?" I asked.

The ghost did not reply.

"Who are you talking to?" Thor stood in the doorway.

"The ghost?"

His eyes crinkled. "Is the ghost answering?"

I handed the book to Thor. "Yes. Sort of. What did Mr. Brown say?"

"He'll call me back. Listen—" he crossed his arms over his chest "—we should talk about last night."

"What about last night?" Thus far, today had been awkward and stiff and I wanted our easy repartee back.

Thor rubbed the space between his eyes. "We were both worried and stressed and—"

"I'm sorry," I blurted. "I shouldn't have yelled at you."

"I shouldn't have yelled at you either."

We stared at each other.

"*Yip*." There was hope for us yet.

The silence between us stretched like the saltwater taffy sold in those horrible shops on Canal Street—but longer and twistier.

I wasn't sure how I felt about him. When we'd danced together I'd felt...something. When I thought he'd been hurt, I'd felt like a bottomless pit had unexpectedly opened beneath my feet. I wasn't ready to feel that way. Not now. Also, spending the next week tiptoeing around each other would be miserable. "I'm not sure last night was—"

"I'm not sure either."

"*Yip*." We were idiots after all.

Thor's phone rang.

I never saw a man answer a call so quickly. "Stone."

He listened.

"Brown," he mouthed.

Mr. Brown spoke loud enough that I caught every third word and each of them had four letters.

"What's wrong?" I whispered.

Thor held up his hand. The expression on his face was grave. "She's right here, sir." Then he held out the phone to me.

Uh-oh. I closed my fingers around Thor's cell. "Mr. Brown?"

"Tell me what exactly what happened on St. Charles."

"Vic Klein's car hit a post. He got out of the car and ran into the Columns Hotel. The men chasing him opened fire on the hotel and Klein escaped out the back. He hid in the car I was driving. I crashed the car—"

"I know that part. You're sure John Howard was one of those men?"

"He was their leader."

Another string of curses had me holding the phone away from my ear. When Mr. Brown paused for breath, I asked, "What's wrong, sir?"

"John Howard is a federal agent."

"He can't be."

"He is."

"What agency?"

"DEA." The Drug Enforcement Agency. It made sense that a DEA agent would be pursuing Vic Klein. What didn't make sense was a federal agent opening fire on a veranda full of innocent people—killing innocent people—then driving away.

"I'm sending you his picture right now."

I crossed the room and dug out my phone.

Seconds later, notification of an email received flashed across my screen.

"Hold on." I opened the email and found John Howard's brown gaze staring up at me. "It's him."

"Do you know what this means, Miss Fields?"

I really didn't. "No." My voice was small.

"It means we've got an agent who's gone bad. Could be he's working for Diaz. If he is, you're in danger."

An understatement. Javier Diaz wanted me dead. "Oh." My voice was even smaller.

"You got that right."

Chapter Twelve

"Put Stone back on the phone." Mr. Brown had nothing more to say to me.

Numbly, I handed Thor's cell back to him.

He held the phone to his ear and watched me sink onto the nearest couch.

While I didn't think Javier Diaz was actively hunting me, I also didn't think he'd pass up the chance to have me killed if the opportunity presented itself. A crooked DEA agent who I'd witnessed committing a murder seemed like a legit opportunity.

I leaned back against the couch, closed my eyes, and half-listened as Thor talked to Mr. Brown. The two speculated where we might look for Mason Hubbard.

The half of me not listening to Thor wondered about the conversation between Quint Arnaut and John Howard. What had they discussed? Did Quint know John Howard was dirty?

"Miss Fields?"

I opened my eyes.

Ladybug stood in the doorway. "May I speak with you, please?"

"Of course." I pushed off the couch and followed her into the hallway. "What is it?"

"Rose O'Leary thinks someone wants her dead. She's scared. Scared to go home. Scared to go to her mother's." Ladybug glanced down at the hands she held clasped together. "Could she stay here for a few days? Until the police sort out this mess?"

Offering James's home as a safe haven was a no-brainer. He made his living saving women on the silver screen. Saving one for real—even if it was just offering a secure place to lay her head—would appeal to him. I nodded my agreement. "Why does Rose think someone wants her dead?"

"She wouldn't say."

Did she know what Mason Hubbard knew? "Where is she?"

"At a table at Pat O'Brien's. She's afraid to leave."

"I'll go get her."

"You?" Ladybug glanced toward the living room and Thor, who was tall and strong and heroic.

Maybe I wasn't looking my toughest in the seersucker sundress Lillian had put me in for the picnic, but looks could be deceiving. "Me."

I couldn't take Thor. The person following him would know Rose was with us—the opposite of hiding her.

"It'll be fine," I promised.

Ladybug did not look convinced.

Thor stuck his head into the hallway. "What's up?"

"You're going praline shopping again," I told him.

"Where are you going?"

"Pat O'Brien's."

"Didn't the doctor tell you not to drink?"

"Very funny. Rose O'Leary is there."

"Who?"

"The singer from last night."

"And?"

"She thinks someone is trying to kill her."

His face tightened. "So you're going to hang out?" Sarcasm. From Thor.

I glanced at Ladybug. "I'm bringing her back here."

Thor glanced at Ladybug too. "You talked to her?"

Ladybug nodded and wrung her hands.

"Do you think she's scared or is someone really trying to kill her?"

Ladybug wrung harder. "Both. She said someone was watching her apartment."

Thor settled his gaze on me. "We should both go."

"You have a tail."

Ladybug's face scrunched in confusion.

Thor crossed his arms. "It's too dangerous for you to go alone."

I glared up at him. "What happened to 'Poppy is more capable than people give her credit for'?"

Thor's lips thinned. "I hate it when you use my words against me."

"Well. Besides, what are the chances someone wants to kill Rose?"

"Someone did shoot up the bar last night." It was a reasonable point.

"Given who was in the bar, the odds they were aiming at Rose are tiny." I turned to Ladybug. "Did Rose say why she thought someone wanted her dead?"

Ladybug, whose poor hands were red from all the wringing, shook her head.

Thor scowled.

I scowled back at him.

His face softened first. He reached out and touched my cheek. "I do think you're capable—I know you're capable—but it's hard to protect yourself from an unknown shooter."

I stepped back—away from the feel of his fingers on my skin. "It's hard for Rose too. Are you going to pick up some pralines?"

Thor answered with an exasperated sigh. "Give me five minutes. I'll call when I get to Jackson Square." He strode to the front door and paused. "If you're not here when I get back, I'm looking for you."

My heart fluttered. "I'll count on it."

A few minutes later, when Thor's number flashed on my screen, I turned to Ladybug. "Call Rose and let her know I'm coming." I slipped out the front door and headed to St. Peter Street. The heels of my shoes clacked against the banquette as I hurried the short distance toward New Orleans' most famous bar.

No one followed me into Pat O'Brien's brick entryway, but I lingered. Had that guy in the Saints hat been behind me since Royal Street?

He leaned against the wall of the voodoo shop across the street and lit a cigarette.

I waited. And waited. But he didn't budge.

Finally, I turned away. Ladybug had told me there were two entrances, this corridor that led to a patio and a restaurant on Bourbon Street. Rose and I could exit through the Bourbon Street entrance and he wouldn't see us leaving.

Assuming I could find her. The sound of lots of people talking and laughing stretched the length of the brick passageway. To my left there was a long narrow bar. I stuck my head inside.

"This is the locals' bar. The courtyard's that way," said a

man sitting on a barstool near the door. He pointed the way with his middle finger.

Well, then.

The courtyard was surrounded by mellow brick walls and filled with glass-top tables, green umbrella shades, and people. So many people. All of whom seemed to be having a splendid time drinking rum in the sunshine.

Where was Rose?

I wound my way through the tables to the bar.

"What can I get you?" asked the bartender.

"I'm looking for someone."

The bartender looked out over the crowded patio and said nothing.

"She's local." Many of the people crowding the patio looked like tourists. They all had Hurricanes in front of them. And most of them looked as if the drinks they now held weren't their first. "Her name is Rose O'Leary. Do you know her?"

"Yeah. I know Rose."

"Where is she?"

"Who wants to know?"

The bartender didn't look like the type to be impressed by Hollywood or fame or pretty women—I briefly wished I'd brought Thor. "Ladybug sent me to get her."

"Ladybug Jenkins?"

I nodded. "Yes."

"Rose is sitting by the fountain."

"Thank you."

I walked toward the fountain, scanning tables as I went. There. A young woman sat alone—well, alone except for two empty glasses. Her eye makeup was slightly smudged. Her hair was slightly messy. Her eyes were slightly glassy. Her face wore the slack expression of someone on the edge of very drunk.

I lifted my sunglasses. "Rose? I'm Poppy. Did Ladybug call you?"

Rose bit her lip and nodded. Slowly. "I saw you last night."

"My friend Mark and I were at the Tiger's Eye when everything—"

"When everything went to hell."

That was as good a way to describe it as any.

"May I sit?"

Using the tip of a black Doc Marten embroidered with roses and decorated with sequin hearts, she pushed out a chair. "So, your mom is a movie star?"

There was no response to that. I sat without replying.

"The guy you were with was gorgeous."

"No argument."

"He ran after the shooter."

I nodded.

"That was totally brave."

Or very stupid. Tomato, tomahto. "I suppose so." I glanced around the patio. Everyone seemed to be having a great time. Except Rose. And me. For us, the laughter and fun could have been a million miles away. "Do you want to tell me what's going on?"

"Pat O's is always crowded, so I figured I'd be safer here than if I was alone."

She wasn't wrong. But that didn't explain why she felt as if she was in danger. "And?"

"I realized I couldn't stay here forever—especially not with that guy watching me—so I asked Ladybug for help. She's really good in a crisis."

Wardrobes. Rescues. Lord knew what else.

But there were more important things to discuss. "Which guy?"

She shot a quick glance to her left. "That one by the door. The guy in the Tigers shirt."

A short muscle-bound man wearing a yellow shirt with purple lettering—Geaux Tigers—leaned against the wall next to the entrance to the Bourbon Street dining room.

"Ladybug told me someone was watching your apartment. Is that the same guy?" I leaned forward. "Have you noticed anyone else watching you?"

"Not the same guy. The guy at my apartment was bigger." Now Rose glanced around the patio. "As for anyone else watching, I don't know."

I let my gaze travel the crowd too. The guy with the Saints hat lurked near the passageway back to St. Peter Street. He and the guy in the Tigers shirt exchanged a glance.

Perfect—they were somehow in this together.

As I watched, Geaux Tigers took out his cell and clicked a picture of me. If he recognized me, and if—when—Rose and I got out of here, it wouldn't be hard for him to figure out where I'd taken her.

Not that his knowing mattered much.

Rose would still be safe at James's. Ever since a crazed stalker broke into his house in Beverly Hills and waited for him in his bed, James made sure his homes were as impenetrable as Fort Knox.

But how were we going to get to James's house? If we simply walked out, Saints and Geaux Tigers would follow us. And there remained the other, bigger question. "Why is Geaux Tigers following you?"

Her teeth worried her lip and she looked down at the empty glasses. "I don't know."

"I think you do."

She jerked her gaze from her lap to my face. "He's just following me."

"Does this have anything to do with Mason Hubbard?"

The color in her face drained away and her eyes widened. "How did you know?"

Lucky guess. "Where is Mason?"

She returned her gaze to her lap and shook her head.

Of course she couldn't just tell me. That would have been too easy. "You need to tell me everything, then I'll call us a cab."

"No!" Rose's hand shot across the table and grabbed my wrist. "No cabs."

"Why not?"

"Mason got into a cab and I haven't seen or heard from him since." Tears welled in her eyes. "It's not like him to disappear. I am not getting in a cab."

"Okay. No cabs."

How were we going to get home safely?

Two women, one of them three sheets, would be no match for them if the men following us attempted to grab Rose. I might be able to take care of one of the guys, but while I was doing that, the other guy could have Rose shoved in a car—or worse.

Besides, what if there were more men in the streets?

We could wait for Thor, but there was no telling how many praline stores he'd visit. Also, giving the men watching us time to call reinforcements seemed like a bad idea. Rose and I ought to leave sooner rather than later.

I listened to the water in the fountain burble and splash, and thought. Hard.

Mr. Brown had hired me because I was recognizable—because no one would expect Poppy Fields to be more than a bit of fluff. And fluff was easy to underestimate. Now was the time for fluff.

I took off my sunglasses, ran my fingers through my hair, and perused the patio. I bestowed smiles on large single men.

The kind who looked like they'd stand up for women they didn't know.

The first two guys to approach us were perfect. They were the approximate size of log cabins. And just as solid.

"Hi," I breathed up at them. "Would you like to join us?"

They settled into the two remaining chairs at the table.

"I'm Billy Bouchet," said the one with darker hair.

"Poppy. And this is my friend Rose."

"I'm Ray." Ray's hair was a soft brown and he possessed serious gray eyes.

"Nice meeting you, Ray."

Rose simply stared at me.

"What are you girls drinking?" Billy waved at a passing waiter.

"I'll get the drinks," I replied.

Billy's eyebrows rose.

"I insist. You see, I'm going to ask you for a favor."

"A favor?"

The waiter, who wore a kelly green jacket with white piping, stopped at our table.

"How big is this favor?" asked Billy.

"Big."

"Elmer T. Lee," Billy told the waiter. "Neat."

"A shot of Patron Platinum," said Ray.

"For you, miss?"

"Just a glass of iced tea, please," I said.

"Sweet?"

"Plain if you've got it."

"I'll have another vodka soda." Not the best idea, but Rose wore a mulish expression—she might not appreciate my thoughts on the importance of sobriety when Saints and Geaux Tigers were following us.

The waiter headed back to the bar.

Billy loosened a slow grin. "Now, what's this favor?"

I took a breath—lying wasn't my best thing. "Rose's ex-boyfriend is following her. We were hoping you could walk us home."

"You didn't need to buy us drinks to get us to do that." I'd been right about Billy. He was a good guy.

I looked up and told the truth. "He can get violent."

Billy cast a sympathetic grin Rose's way. "Not with us around. We'll keep you safe."

The waiter brought our drinks and I handed him a credit card. "I'll take the check and any tab these gentlemen have running."

"You don't need to do that," said Ray.

"I want to. You're doing us a huge favor." I squeezed lemon into my tea and took a small sip. The sugar made my teeth hurt.

"Thanks, Poppy." Billy smiled at me as if he thought my story about Rose's violent ex was an elaborate pick-up line. "Where are you from?"

"California."

"What brings you to New Orleans?"

"A friend's wedding." I glanced at Rose, who'd wrapped her hands tightly around her fresh drink—as if she feared someone might take it from her.

"What about you, Rose?" asked Billy. "Where are you from?"

Rose looked at him as if she didn't understand the question.

I kicked Rose and jerked my chin at Geaux Tigers. His gaze was still fixed on our table.

"I'm local," she said. "What about you?"

"We're from Tennessee." Ray leaned back in his chair. "A buddy's getting married and we're here for the bachelor party."

"What do you do back home?" I asked.

Billy tilted his face toward the sunshine. "We're firemen."

At least they were used to danger.

The waiter came back and I signed the credit card slip.

"Are you girls in a hurry to get home?" Billy coupled his question with a slow smile—an it-would-be-oh-so-much-more-fun-to-linger-on-this-sun-dappled-patio smile.

"We are." I let my tone apologize for us. "When we finish these drinks, we should go."

"Fine, but only if you promise to give me your number."

"She's Poppy Fields," Rose blurted.

Billy's brows rose. "Poppy Fields? Should I know that name?"

Rose nodded. "She's famous."

"For what?" asked Billy.

That stumped her. For about three seconds. "She got abducted by a drug lord."

He scrunched his eyes and shook his head as if Rose were slightly crazy—more than slightly.

"Her mother just saved Paris."

"Her mother?"

"Chariss Carlton."

Billy—and Ray—turned and stared at me. I knew that stare. They were already creating the stories they'd tell their friends when they got home.

Maybe they could tell the story about how they saved me from Rose's jealous ex. "Are we about ready?"

"This is sipping whiskey, not a shot."

I bit my tongue. Rose better know something to help Thor find Mason Hubbard—

otherwise, this afternoon was nothing but a whole lot of aggravation.

Twenty minutes later, Ray helped Rose out of her chair and we walked toward the passageway to St. Peter Street.

Saints stood up straighter as we approached.

Geaux Tigers followed us.

Goody.

The passageway seemed especially dark after sitting on the sunlit patio. I glanced behind us.

Saints and Geaux Tigers were both behind us, and even in the dim light, Saints' grin gleamed.

Uh-oh. With the addition of Billy and Ray, I'd evened the playing field. Saints shouldn't be smiling. Unless he knew something I didn't.

I walked faster.

We emerged onto St. Peter and I scanned the street.

Three additional men loitered on the banquette.

Hopefully Billy and Ray were as solid as they looked.

Hopefully the bad guys didn't have guns.

I should have thought of that before I asked Billy and Ray to help us.

"Which way?" asked Billy.

"Right. Toward the river."

We walked about five steps and Ray asked, "Does your ex have a bunch of friends?" He must have noticed the five men following us.

Rose's grip on his arm tightened.

We were so close to Royal Street, and from there it was only a short distance to James's.

"Hey!"

I pretended I didn't hear and kept walking.

A hand closed on my arm and yanked. "I'm talking to you."

I spun around. "Let go of me."

Saints' lips twitched as if I'd amused him.

"Or what?"

"Let go of the lady." Billy loomed behind me.

"This isn't your fight, dude."

"I said let her go."

It was hard to breathe with all the testosterone in the air.

I jerked my arm out of Saints' grasp and his mouth formed an O of surprise.

"The best thing you could do," I told him, "is let us go."

"Not gonna happen." His gaze took in my stance—feet apart, knees slightly bent, ready—then traveled to Rose, who was looking at us with an expression of horror on her face. She clutched Ray with one hand. The other she pressed against her stomach.

Saints and Geaux Tigers moved toward her.

And Rose threw up on their shoes.

Chapter Thirteen

Rose vomited with wild abandon. Pea soup abandon.

Twin looks of disgust graced Saints' and Geaux Tigers' faces and they jumped back. Way back.

Ray hardly reacted. As a firefighter, he'd probably seen much worse than Rose losing multiple vodka sodas on the flagstone banquette.

Rose looked up with bleary eyes and wiped her mouth with the back of her hand.

"Can you carry her?" I asked Ray.

"No problem." He picked her up, tossed her over his shoulder, and raced toward Royal Street.

Billy and I followed them.

"Put me down!" Rose beat against Ray's back. "I'm gonna throw up again."

Ray ignored her request. And her warning.

"At least slow down," she begged.

Ray ignored that too.

I risked a glance behind us. Saints and Geaux Tigers were

still wiping their shoes on the curb while the additional men laughed at them.

Ray rounded Royal Street and turned left.

"Wait!" I called after him. "The house is the other way."

But Ray didn't wait. Or slow down. Or give any indication he'd heard me.

"Ray!" I yelled. "We need to go the other way."

Ray ignored me as easily as he'd ignored Rose.

"Where is he—" The feel of a muzzle against my back rendered me mute.

Seriously?

"Keep going," said Billy.

"I bought your drinks." What kind of a kidnapper lets his victim pick up his bar tab?

The kind who kidnapped an idiot.

With the gun pressed against my back, I followed Ray and Rose. A few of the people on the banquette raised their brows, but most acted as if seeing a woman in a fireman's hold was no big deal.

And Rose wasn't objecting.

After her initial complaints, she just hung there, limp as a strand of over-cooked linguini.

"Who do you work for?" I asked.

Billy dug the gun further into my back.

Okay. No questions. I got it.

We were a block from Jackson Square, one of the busiest places in New Orleans. All I needed was to get us there.

I stumbled on the banquette and fell to my knees. The pressure of the gun on my back disappeared and I screamed, "Help! They've drugged my friend. We're being kidnapped!"

Billy grabbed my arm and yanked me off the pavers.

But he was too late.

The people who'd been ignoring us now stared.

"My wife has had too much to drink."

"I'm not his wife. I'm Poppy Fields. Google me."

Around us, people looked down at their phones.

"She is Poppy Fields," said a woman wearing a fanny pack. She held up her phone. "I recognize her from the news."

Billy had a windbreaker draped over his gun. I tugged at the sleeve. "His friend is kidnapping my friend Rose." With my free hand, I pointed at Ray's disappearing back.

The small crowd around us seemed too stunned to move—except for an ennui-filled teenager who filmed us on her cell. She shifted her camera and caught Ray dashing down Pirate Alley.

I tugged harder on Billy's windbreaker and the coat fell off his arm.

"Gun!" someone screamed.

More screams. And running. And even more screaming.

I clenched my hand into a fist and drove my elbow deep into Billy's unsuspecting midsection.

He grunted.

I whirled and poked at his eyes.

Billy dropped the gun to the banquette and grabbed—blindly—for my hands.

I kicked the gun out into the street and rammed my knee into the place Billy least wanted to feel it.

Now Billy dropped to the banquette.

I ran down Pirate Alley. To my left lay a garden and then the walls of the cathedral. To my right stretched neat buildings with closed shutters. Beneath my feet were uneven flagstones and a shallow divot for rainwater. Nowhere were Ray or Rose.

I burst into Jackson Square.

There were artists and buskers, a fortuneteller and a living statue. Scents carried from the river. I heard the whinny of horses, the notes of a saxophone, the gentle rustle of a breeze through the palm fronds, bits and pieces of conversation.

Ray and Rose were gone.

I ran toward Decatur, my heels and the rasp of my breath adding to the sounds in the square.

No sign of them.

Where could he have taken her?

Anywhere.

My shoulders sagged. I'd promised to bring Rose to safety. Instead, I'd delivered her to the hands of—who? Billy could tell me.

I ran back to Royal Street.

The little crowd that had watched me take Billy down was still there—still buzzing.

But Billy wasn't.

"Where did he go?" I asked.

"He hopped in a car," said a helpful bald man. "I took a picture."

I glanced down at the phone he held out to me. The man had captured part of a Louisiana plate, complete with a pelican and the words "Sportsman's Paradise." I memorized the letters —PKX 1. Too bad he'd missed the numbers that came next.

"Did you find your friend?" asked the teen who'd been taping.

"No."

"I've got the video. I can send it to you."

At that moment, a NOPD cruiser pulled to the curb next to us and two police officers wearing familiar buff blue uniform shirts climbed out and surveyed the gathering of stunned people.

I rushed forward. "My friend has been kidnapped."

"I got video," volunteered the girl with the cell. All of her ennui had disappeared with the arrival of the police, and she seemed eager to help.

"Your name?" asked the older of the two officers.

"She's Poppy Fields," said the girl. "And I'm Lola, Lola Lapin."

The officer looked at me more closely. "Poppy Fields?"

I nodded. "I was at the Columns on Thursday." Reminding the officers I'd saved one of their own seemed like a good idea.

And it worked. The police officer's expression softened from what-fresh-hell-is-this to how-can-I-help. "What happened here?"

"Rose O'Leary's been kidnapped."

"The singer?"

"I got the video!" Lola shoved her cell under our noses and we watched Ray run down Pirate Alley with Rose draped over his shoulder. The camera swung back to me jamming my fingers in Billy's eye.

The officer grunted in sympathy when my knee connected with Billy's groin.

Lola filmed me running down Pirate Alley instead of Billy's reaction to being beat up by a girl—or disappearing.

"What happened to the guy?" he asked.

"He got in a car and drove off," said one of the onlookers.

"Anybody have a description of the car?"

It was dark blue. It was dark gray. It was a Nissan or Honda or Kia.

"That man got a shot of the license plate." I searched the crowd for the bald man who'd showed me the picture, but he'd disappeared. "Where did he go?"

"Who?" asked Lola.

"The bald man who took the picture."

"He took off as soon as the police pulled up," she replied.

The police officer stepped into the center of the little crowd. "Did anyone else take pictures or video?"

If anyone did, they kept quiet about it.

After a moment of silence, the older officer looked over to the younger one. "Get names and contact information." He turned to Lola and me. "Miss Fields, Miss Lapin, you'll need to come to the station."

"What about Rose?"

"Our best chance of finding her is analyzing the video."

"What about the license plate number?" I asked.

"The guy with the picture is gone."

"But I memorized part of the plate. PKX 1."

"Louisiana plates?"

I nodded.

"I'll call it in." He waved us toward the car.

While we buckled, he spoke into the radio, "I've got a partial on a Louisiana plate. PKX 1." Then he put the car in gear and drove us to the police station.

When we arrived, Detective Langlois opened my car door and spoke over me. "Where'd you get that plate number, Mike?"

The officer—Mike—glanced my way. "Miss Fields gave it to me."

Now Detective Langlois settled his gaze on me. "Are you sure about those numbers?"

"Positive. Why?"

"You ever heard of a guy named Lyman Cox?"

"I met him last night."

"It's possible the car belongs to him." He extended a hand.

I thought for a moment before I placed my fingers in his palm. Why would Lyman Cox have Rose kidnapped? "I bet when you call, someone will discover the car's been stolen."

Detective Langlois glanced at Lola. "Miss Fields, it's time you and I talk."

I followed the detective into an office and stopped to look at the photographs hanging on the walls. "Your brothers?" I nodded toward a shot of three men in hunting gear.

"Yep."

"Your mother had her hands full."

"She did." He sank into the chair behind a desk covered in paperwork. "You want to tell me what's going on?"

More than anything. There was no way I could find Rose by myself. But I couldn't tell him anything. Not without Mr. Brown's permission. And Mr. Brown took secrecy seriously. "May I make a call?"

"By all means, Miss Fields, chat with friends."

I gave Detective Langlois the chilly look his comment deserved, pulled my phone out of my bag, and dialed Mr. Brown.

"What is it, Miss Fields?" The long-suffering Mr. Brown had girded himself for my latest disaster.

"I'm in Detective Langlois's office."

"What happened?" Whatever the disaster was, he'd bend his shoulder and clean up the mess.

"A woman—a friend of the man you sent Mark to see—was abducted." I took a breath. "While I was with her."

"Where's Stone?"

Shopping for pralines wasn't a good answer. "Pursuing another lead."

"What is it you want from me, Miss Fields?" He didn't much like all this girding and bending. In fact, he had Poppy fatigue.

"I want to tell the police detective the truth. A woman's life might be at stake."

Mr. Brown's sigh reached all the way to his toes. "His name?

I glanced at the detective. "René Langlois."

"I'll call you back in ten minutes. In the meantime, tell him nothing. Got it?"

"Got it." I hung up the phone.

"Something to tell me?"

"I can't."

"Can't or won't?"

"Can't. I'm waiting for permission."

"There's more to you than meets the eye."

"Isn't that true of most people?"

"Hardly. Most people—there's less to them than meets the eye."

"Is anyone looking for Rose?"

"Everyone's looking for Rose."

Except me. I was sitting in a chair waiting on Mr. Brown.

"Is there anything you can tell me?"

I thought. "The guy I took down in the video. He said his name was Billy Bouchet."

Detective Langlois's fingers flew across a keyboard. "Remind me not to get on your bad side."

"Don't abuse my generosity."

The arch of Detective Langlois's brow asked the question.

"He let me pay his liquor bill, then stuck a gun in my back."

The detective—René—chuckled. "You sound more upset about the bar tab."

"It's the principle of the—"

René's face had gone cop-like. Serious. Worried. "What do you know about the recent shootings, Miss Fields?"

I shook my head. I couldn't tell him.

"I'm with the police."

"Until I hear back—" I glanced down at the silent cell in my lap "—I can't say a word."

"I could charge you."

"With what?"

"Withholding evidence."

"Is that a real charge?"

He grimaced and turned his monitor. "Is this the guy?"

Billy's face filled the screen.

"That's him."

"Billy Bouchet. He got picked up for dealing when he was in college. Looks like he's graduated to something bigger."

"His friend's name was Ray."

"Did you get a last name?"

"No. But can't you search for known associates?"

"Like his fraternity brothers?"

"You just said Billy got picked up for dealing."

"And he was sentenced to a hundred hours of community service."

"For dealing drugs?"

"College kid. First offense." He squinted at the screen. "A small amount of weed. Makes sense. Some judge decided to keep Billy's jail cell open for a serious criminal."

"I'd say he's crossed the line now." I thought about Rose's limp body hung over Ray's shoulder. Had they somehow drugged her? Had they put something in my drink? It was a good thing I hadn't touched my glass after that first cloying taste of sweet tea.

"Does he have anything to do with the shootings?"

"I honestly don't know. He couldn't be behind all this." This—whatever this was—included shipping containers filled with drugs, multiple murders, and corruption. A twenty-something college drug-dealer was not the mastermind.

"So who is?"

That I could answer. "I don't know."

The phone in my lap vibrated, and I tapped the screen. "Hello?"

"Miss Fields, you're on *TMZ*."

"What? Hold on. I'm putting you on speaker." I tapped my way to *TMZ* and watched myself gouge Billy in the eyes, kick his gun into the street, and put him on the pavement with a well-placed knee. It wasn't Lola's video. This footage came from a different angle. When Billy fell, I barely glanced at him—instead, I took off running down Pirate Alley. "Oh." It was the only thing I could think to say.

"Take me off speaker."

I did as I was told. "You're off."

"You are going to explain to that pack of hyenas that follows wherever you go the importance of the self-defense classes you took when you got back from Mexico."

I swallowed. "Okay."

"You will be fluffy." Mr. Brown's voice brooked no arguments. "You will be ditzy." The man was mad as hell. "You will convince people to underestimate you."

"Okay," I replied.

"I'll speak with you lat—"

"What should I tell Detective Langlois?" I rushed through my question.

"Right. Nothing."

"Nothing?" Seriously? Rose had been kidnapped. "But—"

"You'll find you can say a lot without saying anything at all." He hung up.

The ensuing silence spoke volumes.

Detective Langlois clasped his hands and rested them against the surface of his desk. "Who do you work for, Miss Fields?"

"I can't tell you."

"Did you come to New Orleans on behalf of the employer you can't tell me about?"

"I came to New Orleans to be in my friend's wedding."

"And everything that's happened since you arrived—the shootings, the bombing, the kidnapping—just—" he separated his hands and splayed his fingers "—happened?"

I nodded.

"You expect me to believe that?"

"It's the truth."

"You must be the unluckiest young woman alive."

We let that observation hang in the air for a few seconds.

"You're not going to say anything, are you?" He scowled at me.

I shook my head.

"How about if I run a few things by you?"

"I can listen all day."

"The shootings at the Columns and Tiger's Eye are related. Were you a target?"

"I'm here for Adele's wedding. Why would anyone target me?"

Detective Langlois stared at me for long seconds. "The Columns really was bad luck. Worse luck for the guy you saw. And you kept seeing him."

John Howard. The man's name was John Howard.

"Any theories on the bombing, Miss Fields?"

I shook my head again.

"I have a theory. Would you like to hear it?"

I nodded.

"There's more than one player out there. And somehow—bad luck? Bad karma?—you've got yourself caught in the middle."

I swallowed.

"I have a few friends in Washington, Miss Fields. I'll be calling them."

"You should."

"I don't expect immediate answers." He scowled at me. "In the meantime, try not to get yourself killed."

"I'll try."

The phone on his desk rang and he picked up the receiver and listened, his scowl growing more pronounced with each second. "Got it." He hung up and returned his scowl to me. "Your public awaits."

"My public?"

"The press. There are so many of them on the front steps no one can get in or out of the station. What are you going to tell them?"

I didn't talk to the press. Not if I could help it. And there was no better way to undermine a perception of toughness than by letting a man do my talking for me. "Maybe you could do the talking?"

"Me?"

"Just tell them that after my ordeal in Mexico I took self-defense classes. Make it about finding Rose."

Detective Langlois just stared at me.

"Please?"

Detective Langlois's expression didn't change. Much. A gleam appeared in his eyes.

"What do you want?"

"Answers."

The one thing I couldn't give him. "I'll move heaven and earth to get clearance to tell you everything."

The detective answered me with a curt nod and pushed out his chair.

A barrage of questions met us when we stepped out of the police station.

Detective Langlois answered them all.

"Poppy!"

I recognized the voice and my spine stiffened. What was he doing here?

I located the man in the crowd

He grinned at me. Grinned. A sunny, lazy grin that had me grinding my teeth.

Some of the reporters followed my gaze, and Jake was forced to ask a question. "How do you know Rose O'Leary?"

"I'm a huge fan of her music."

I inched closer to Detective Langlois, went so far as to rest my hand on his arm, as if answering one question had drained me.

The detective took the hint. "That'll be all."

He ignored the reporters' pleas and led me back into the station. "I'll drive you home."

"Thank you."

We were almost to James's house before Detective Langlois said anything. "That was a nice thing you did back there. For Rose."

"You sound surprised."

"I guess I am."

I stared straight out the windshield. "I'd tell you everything if I could."

He parked the car in front of James's door.

I wrapped my fingers around the door handle and glanced at the house. It was only a matter of time before the paparazzi figured out where I was staying but, for now, I had the banquette to myself.

"Thanks for the ride, Detective. Will you keep me posted? Please?"

He nodded. Once. Then he reached in his jacket and pulled out a gun—my gun. "You may need this."

I took the gun, placed it into my purse, and opened the door. "Thank you."

"Miss Fields..."

I paused.

"When you go looking for Rose, try not to shoot anyone."

"I'll try."

I dashed across the pavement and slipped through the front door.

Ladybug waited for me in the hall. "Thank heavens you're all right. I saw you on the news."

"I'm so sorry." I'd gone to help her friend and made things exponentially worse.

"Sorry?"

"About Rose."

"I'm sorry I nearly got you kidnapped."

"The police will find her." And if they didn't, Thor and I would. "Where's Mark?"

"He's not back yet."

"But I've been gone for hours." What could have happened to him?

Chapter Fourteen

"*Yip*!" Pay attention to me.

I picked up Consuela, buried my nose in her fur, and rested against the wall. "You're sure you haven't heard from him?"

"I'm sure. I thought he was with you."

"*Yip*." How could I have lost someone as big as Thor?

I hadn't lost him, and I knew how to find him. "Here." I handed Consuela to Ladybug, pulled out my cell, and tapped on Thor's contact information. We'd set up tracking when he got his new phone.

The little map on the screen showed Thor was near the river. I breathed a sigh of relief and held the phone out to Ladybug. "Any idea where that is?"

"The port."

Of course it was.

I texted, U okay?

Thor didn't answer.

I'd give him a minute before I worried. "I'm going to change." If I was going to the port to look for Thor, I wasn't wearing a seersucker dress. I reclaimed Consuela and walked toward the stairs. "It's possible a friend may show up. His name is Jake Smith. If he arrives before I'm ready, he can wait in the living room." I climbed three stairs and paused again. "If he arrives with luggage, put him in the bedroom farthest from mine."

I went to my room, shucked off the dress, and pulled on a pair of black pants and a tee-shirt. My feet I slipped into so-comfortable-I-could-run-a-mile-in-them Tod's loafers. There was nothing bright, ruffled, floral, or monogrammed on my whole body. And that was fine by me.

I checked my phone—no return text—and descended the stairs.

Jake stuck his head out of the living room. "You okay?

"*Grrr.*"

Consuela had read my mind. I had every reason to be annoyed with Jake. Every reason. "I'm glad you're here."

"You are?" The surprise on his face was fleeting, replaced by a slow grin. "Of course you are."

"Ego much?"

Thunk!

"What was that?" Jake looked over his shoulder into the living room.

I breezed past him. "The ghost."

"The ghost?" Disbelief colored his voice.

I slipped behind the couch, put Consuela down, and picked up the volume on the floor. *Paradise Lost.* I handed Jake the book. "This one's for you."

He winced. "A ghost, you say?"

"Yep."

"Maybe paradise isn't lost. You just said you were glad to see me."

"Because Mark's in trouble."

"Stone? Stone doesn't get into trouble."

"He does today."

"Where is he?"

"The port."

"Is he investigating a lead?"

"I don't know."

"Have you called him?"

I didn't need to call Thor to know he was in trouble. If he was all right, he would have come looking for me hours ago. And he would have returned my text. But because Jake was watching—and smirking—I called.

Thor didn't answer.

After six rings, I hung up.

"How do you know he's at the port?"

"We're tracking each other's phones."

Jake's eyes narrowed slightly. "So really, all you know is Stone's phone is at the port. He could have lost it, or this could be a trap."

"A trap?"

Jake nodded. "Mr. Brown filled me in. Some very dangerous people want you out of the way."

"How could he know that?"

Jake didn't answer.

I took a breath. A deep one. "It would be nice if Mr. Brown would fill me in."

"Consider me his emissary. And I'm not letting you walk into a trap."

"*Yip.*" Much as she hated to admit it, Jake had a point.

"That won't happen."

"How can you be so sure?"

I smiled up at him. "Because I have backup."

"What exactly is your plan?"

"I go to the port, find Mark, and, if he needs rescuing, I rescue him. You're my backup."

"That's a terrible plan. How about I go to the port and haul Stone's ass out of the sling? You stay here."

Jake and I had fallen apart because he didn't think I was cut out for anything more taxing than dancing at the latest hottest club till three in the morning. I'd proved him wrong. Twice. But he still had some crazy idea about protecting me. I crossed my arms. "Not gonna happen. Besides, my plan is better. Even if it is a trap, they won't be expecting you."

"They won't be expect—"

"I'm sorry to interrupt," said Ladybug. "But Mama Vielle is on the phone for you, Miss Fields."

I glanced at the phone next to the couch. "I'll take it in the study."

As I stalked out of the room with Consuela at my heels, Ladybug said, "I've put your things in the back bedroom, Mr. Smith."

I gave her an approving smile.

Jake, unable to take the most basic hint, followed me into James's pecan-paneled study. "I thought you wanted to go to the port. Who is this Mama Vielle?"

"The voodoo priestess who saved my life last night."

That shut him up.

I picked up the receiver. "Hello."

"I saw you on the news." Mama Vielle sounded tired and weak.

"How are you feeling?"

"Like ten miles of bad road, but I didn't call to talk about me."

"You need to concentrate on getting better."

"You need to tell me what's going on."

"They took Rose. And I think they have my friend Mark."

"The man you were with last night?"

Jake flopped into a leather club chair and picked up a crystal egg.

I turned my back on him. "That's him."

"He's a fine-looking man."

"He is."

"Got any idea who took them?"

"It's going to sound crazy, but I think there are two different groups of bad guys. I'm not sure if Rose and Mark were taken by the same groups."

Mama Vielle's cackle had the hair on the back of my neck standing straight up. "You're smarter than people give you credit for. I reckon you're right. There's a whole mess of darkness slinking through the streets. You still got that hoodoo I gave you?

"I do." It was tucked safely in my purse.

"You keep it with you."

"I will."

"You going after him?"

"I am." I glanced over my shoulder at Jake. He was picking at one of the chair's leather buttons and pretending not to listen.

"I figured as much. You watch out for a man in a yellow hat."

He should be easy to spot. "What man?"

"Don't know. It's something the spirits whispered in my ear."

I had no response for that.

"Poppy?"

"I'm here, Mama Vielle."

"When you're done saving that man of yours, you come see me."

"I will."

"And bring him with you. I could use something good to look at."

"I promise."

"Be careful."

I was left with a dial tone. I hung up the phone and glanced at Jake, who was busy pretending to examine his cuticles. "After I grab my handbag, we're good to go."

"I thought we agreed you're not going."

"You agreed. I did not."

We stared at each other. Neither willing to cede an inch.

"You do realize I can go without you?"

Jake deflated. "You're carrying a handbag on a rescue mission?"

"I am." I wasn't telling Jake about the hoodoo—he'd only make fun. And I wasn't carrying the smelly little bundle on my body. I smoothed my tee-shirt. "Guns are so bulky."

Jake rolled his eyes. "How are we getting there?"

"We're driving. What? What's that look?"

Jake's lips were drawn back from his teeth. "I've driven with you."

"I'm a good driver."

"No, you're not."

"You never complained when we were dating."

"We were dating. Of course I didn't."

One little fender bender with a lawnmower and all of a sudden I was a bad driver. It was a good thing Jake didn't know what I'd done to Adele's Porsche. "Fine. You can drive." I reached into my pocket and tossed him the key.

I refused to respond to Jake's grin when he saw the rearing horse on the fob. I merely walked, with my held high, to the stairs. "I'm going to ask Ladybug to keep an eye on Consuela. I'll be ready in two minutes."

When Jake slid into the driver's seat, he flexed his fingers before wrapping them around the wheel. "Nice car."

"Try not to wreck it," I snapped.

Jake pulled out onto Royal Street. "You're the one who totaled a lawnmower."

"It was parked too close to the curb."

"Do you hear yourself?"

"It wasn't my fault."

His gaze lingered on me for far too long, and I didn't care for the smirk on his lips. "So the lawnmower was to blame?"

He never gave me credit for missing the person pushing the lawnmower. I turned on the stereo and music surrounded us. "That's Boozoo Chavis." I recognized the song.

"Who?"

"Boozoo Chavis. He's a zydeco legend."

He side-eyed me. "What's happened to you?"

"What do you mean?"

"You've been here three days and you're talking about ghosts and voodoo priestesses and zydeco."

"There are a lot of things about me you don't know."

"I know you better than you think. I know you should go back to California. Sit on the beach. Enjoy life. Stay safe."

My jaw tightened. "Go to hell, Jake."

After that, we didn't talk. We just drove.

Three whole minutes of nothing but zydeco.

"Where exactly are we going?" he asked.

I opened the map on my phone and stared at Thor's little blue dot. It hadn't moved. "Looks like the corner of Henderson and Port of New Orleans Place."

"We get one drive-by."

Only one chance to observe what I might be walking into? "One?"

"You're sure something has happened to Stone?"

"He would have come looking for me if he was okay."

Jake nodded as if he agreed with my assessment. "We get one pass. This car isn't exactly inconspicuous."

Adele's ringtone startled us both and I fumbled for the phone in my lap. "Hey."

"Are you all right? Momma saw you on the six o'clock news."

"I'm fine, but I'm so glad we've got the evening off." There were—amazingly—no parties that night.

"Me too. But I'm worried about you. Should I come over?" That would be a problem.

"Don't you dare. Put your feet up and relax. I'm fine."

"What happened?"

"It's a long story and I—"

"What's that growling sound/"

"The car. We ran out to get a bite to eat."

"Liar," Jake whispered.

"You could come here for dinner," Adele offered.

"Thanks, but it's just a quick bite, then we're headed home, where I'm putting on my jammies and curling up with the remote."

"I wouldn't be."

"What do you mean?"

"I wouldn't put on jammies. Mark is gorgeous. If ever there was a reason for a sexy nightgown, he's it. If I were you, I'd forget about the remote and curl up with him." Adele's voice was loud. Too loud. "The way he looked at you when you were dancing..." She sighed.

Jake's hands tensed on the wheel and his lips thinned.

"Adele, I gotta go. I'll talk to you tomorrow." I hung up.

"You're with Stone now?" Each word was precisely clipped.

"No. I'm not. But if I was, it wouldn't be any of your business."

"Poppy—"

I held up a hand, stopping him. "No, Jake. Not tonight. We can fight after we've rescued Thor."

"Thor? You call him Thor?"

"Not to his face."

He responded with an unreadable expression, but he drove us by the building. Once. The place was enormous.

"What is that place?" I asked.

"That's where they make and store floats for Mardi Gras parades."

"A—how do you know that? B—there's more than one parade?"

"I've been to New Orleans before, Poppy." Jake cast a quick glance my way. "Hasn't your friend told you about krewes?"

"No."

"Ask her."

"How big is it?" Finding Thor would be like finding a single needle in a hundred haystacks.

"Big," Jake replied. "Eighty thousand square feet. Here's what we're gonna do. I'll go in first and if it's clear, I'll—"

"I'll go in first."

"Poppy—"

"Get over yourself, Jake. I'm going in. You're the backup. That means you're in back."

"But—"

"No buts."

Jake tensed—his jaw, his hands on the wheel, his shoulders. He even sat up straighter in his seat. But he drove to a lot full of cars with out-of-state license plates and parked without further comment.

I surveyed the sea of cars. "Isn't this too far away?"

"A Ferrari parked in front of the building would stand out."

"If I'd known you were going to be this fussy, I would have borrowed Ladybug's Malibu."

Jake's scowl was clearly visible in the darkness.

We wove through the cars—Jake told me it was a cruise-ship parking lot—and snuck up next to the building.

"Okay." Jake leaned against the corrugated metal wall and crossed his arms. "Since you insist on being first in, how are you getting inside?"

There were times Jakes deserved every arrow I shot at him. Now was one of those time.

I reached into my handbag and pulled out a bundle of tools.

His brows rose. "Since when do you know how to pick a lock?"

Since one of Chariss's directors had hired a real cat burglar as a consultant on a film. Maurice, bored nearly out of his mind with endless days spent on a movie set, taught me everything he knew. Or at least he tried. Maurice could pick a lock with a hairpin. I needed actual tools.

A moment later, the door was open.

Jake, who obviously expected me to fail, caught my arm. "I don't like this."

"You've made that abundantly clear."

"We don't know what we're up against."

"When has that ever stopped you?"

Jake's fingers swept across my cheek and the look in his eyes was soft. For a half-second I remembered what it was like to be in love with him. "It's not me I'm worried about."

In a rush, I remembered why I stopped loving Jake. He'd treated me like a porcelain doll, lied to me, and broken my heart —all three, more than once. And all because he worried.

"I'll be fine." I slipped inside the dark building.

A woman stood on the other side of the door. She stared at

me, her arms uplifted as if she were calling on the gods to smite me.

My heart battered my chest, my mouth went dry, and I didn't move a muscle.

Neither did she.

We stood there. Immobile. At an impasse.

I ventured a tiny step.

She didn't move. Did she—I squinted in the darkness—have snakes for hair?

She wasn't alive.

She never had been.

I took a deep breath and looked around. Everywhere, faces leered at me from the darkness—Elvis, Marilyn Monroe, court jesters, knights on white horses, elves (the Tolkien variety, not the Keebler kind), leprechauns, flappers, gypsies, pirates, cowboys, and Norse gods. There were fantastical flowers and sea monsters, birds (many of them pelicans), and chests overflowing with treasure.

When the sun was out, the place was probably magical. At night, it was the creepiest spot on the planet.

I tiptoed silently forward, glad my shoes had rubber soles. One small blessing. The impossibility of finding Thor in this giant building filled with a million places to hide nearly overwhelmed me.

All those lifeless eyes—I felt them watching me. And somewhere—human eyes.

Had the people who took Thor heard me come in?

Scritch.

A shudder ran from the roots of my hair to the tips of my painted toenails. What was that sound?

I followed my ears (hard to do with my heartbeat pounding against my eardrums) through the crowded warehouse.

Scriiitch.

Hiding in the deepest shadows, I crept closer to the sound.

Someone had constructed a painting theater and lit it with a single dim lightbulb. Three of the walls were heavy plastic. The floor was covered with a tarp. A thousand different colors dripped and ran. The fourth wall was open to the warehouse. Thor sat in the center, slumped in a chair with his hands tied behind his back. His chin rested on his chest. A trickle of dried blood ran from his hairline to his chin. He wasn't moving.

Remaining where I was—hidden in the shadows—took every bit of willpower I possessed. My heart and my feet told me to run to Thor. I scrunched my eyes closed—I had to be smart about this.

Scritch.

Where was the noise coming from?

I couldn't tell.

I studied the little room and came to three conclusions.

I was the mouse.

Thor was the cheese.

And the little room was a trap.

Chapter Fifteen

I hid behind an enormous monkey, stared at Thor—Mark—and wondered what to do.

I couldn't walk into the trap—someone had obviously left Thor's phone on so I could track him. That or they were idiots. And anyone who could outsmart Thor was definitely not an idiot.

I couldn't call for help, the light from my phone would—

Crap! My phone.

If I'd tracked Thor, whoever built the trap had probably tracked me. They knew I was here.

A chill trickled down my spine.

I squeezed my eyes shut and indulged in regrets.

I should have leveled with Detective Langlois. Barring that, I should have at least asked him for help before racing off like a wild hare with only Jake for backup.

Where was Jake?

I searched the darkness and spotted Lucille Ball. No Jake. But Lucy's smile said she thought my predicament was hilarious.

I slid my hand into my bag and my fingers searched for—that would do.

I pulled out a peppermint and threw the little piece of hard candy to my left.

The candy hit a character whose features were obscured by shadow, then clattered to the floor. In the quiet warehouse, the sound of peppermint meeting poured concrete was as loud as a gunshot.

Thor didn't move.

But three shadows broke away from the darkness and slinked toward the candy.

Three. I had to assume they had guns. I had to assume they'd use them.

I reached into my handbag a second time—my wallet, my phone, my lockpick tools, my gun, Mama Vielle's hoodoo, and a lipstick. I needed something to throw and I had two choices. Hoodoo or lipstick? The lipstick was my favorite—Sisley—in a discontinued color, and couldn't be replaced. But I'd promised Mama Vielle. Swallowing a sigh, I threw the lipstick.

Again to my left, but farther this time.

The clatter when lipstick tube met concrete was deafening.

"*Oomph.*"

Oomph? What had happened? I searched the darkness.

Outsized characters still loomed and leered, but I saw no actual people.

Now or never. I crouched lower and tiptoed away from the monkey, closer to Thor, but my foot caught, and I felt one of the characters—a huge one—begin its descent to the floor.

I ran, as far and as fast and quietly as I could.

The character's crash reverberated through the warehouse.

Even Thor moved.

Which meant he was alive.

The sound of my heartbeat in my ears was nearly as loud as

the crash. I forced breath deep into my lungs, relaxed my tense muscles, and scanned the darkness.

There! Someone crept toward me—an oily, menacing shadow.

I pulled my gun out of my handbag and carefully looped the hobo over my shoulder and around my neck. If I made it through this night, I'd have to write Devi Kroell about how great their bags were for breaking and entering and life-or-death standoffs—the average day.

The shadow veered slightly to my right. Only a vampire separated us.

I shifted my weight and tightened my grip on the gun.

The shadow inched forward.

I raised my arm—and brought my hand down as hard as I could.

Thunk!

The impact from the stock of my gun meeting the shadow's skull shook my bones.

I was running before the shadow hit the floor. I hid in the deep darkness cast by a giant Venus flytrap.

I glanced toward Thor.

He'd lifted his chin and his eyes were narrowed against the light from the tired lightbulb. "Poppy?" His voice was hoarse. "Get out. It's a trap."

Well, duh. Why couldn't he tell me something useful like the number of bad guys?

Now what?

I could walk into the trap and see what happened. A remarkably bad idea.

I could risk the light from my phone and call the police. Much less suicidal, but a sure way to spend the next day or two in an interrogation room.

I could find Jake. An impossibility in the sprawling warehouse.

Or...I crept toward my first hiding spot, the monkey, but the fallen character blocked my way. I skirted around the edges and my foot hit a chunk of whatever the artist used to create it. I bent and picked up the piece—Styrofoam and papier mâché, if its feel in my hand was any indication.

The monkey's shadow offered me cover. I identified my next hiding place, primed myself to run, and took aim at the light bulb.

Bang!

The light above Thor's enclosure exploded. I was already crouched low, running toward a witch's head the size of a small refrigerator, before the glass hit the floor.

Bang!

Behind me, the monkey disintegrated.

My heart might be jackhammering its way out of my chest, but I'd done it. Thor was in the dark. If I went to him, I wouldn't be spotlighted.

I tossed the bit of Styrofoam and papier mâché to my right and listened.

No one reacted when the piece hit the floor. No one made a sound.

If I was lucky, that first *oomph* had been Jake sneaking up on a bad guy. I'd taken out a second. That left one who I knew about. It was time to take the risk.

I crept toward Thor and hit my knee. Hard. "Crap!" I clapped my hand over my mouth, dropped to the floor, and prayed. Nothing. No reaction. It was as if I was alone in the warehouse. I wasn't. And now, everyone knew where I was.

If I ever decided to save someone in a dark warehouse again, I was getting myself night-vision goggles. This banging around in the dark was ridiculous.

I slipped my hand into my bag and eased open a zippered pocket. My fingers closed around my dad's Swiss army knife.

With my heart in my throat, I rose to my feet and crept closer to Thor.

At the edge of the tarp, I paused.

I strained to hear.

Where was Jake?

Was Thor hurt?

Could he walk?

Could he make it all the way to the cruise-ship parking lot where Jake insisted we leave the car?

With the knife in one hand and the gun in the other, I tiptoed onto the tarp.

Five steps took me to Thor. I crouched behind him and sawed at the rope circling his wrists.

Bit by bit, fiber by fiber, the rope gave way.

I held my breath the whole time. My lungs threatened to burst. My heart threatened to jump out of my throat and run away. My fingers shook.

Thor was free. Released, his arms hung limp.

I took air deep into my lungs and tugged his hand. We needed to move. Now.

Thor moved slowly—as if his muscles and bones were stiff from being tied to a chair.

I tugged again. Harder. He could be stiff later. Right now, we needed a fast exit.

Thor stood, stumbled on the tarp, and took us both to the ground.

Bang!

A bullet whizzed above our heads.

"C'mon." I crawled toward the edge of the tarp, willing Thor to follow me. We'd be safer in the general warehouse.

Figures made of Styrofoam and papier mâché might not offer protection, but they'd make spotting us much harder.

Bang!

The bullet was so close to my ear I felt its passage.

Where was Jake?

"Faster." I pulled myself forward using my thighs and forearms.

Bang!

This time the bullet sailed above us.

Thump!

It was the blessed sound of a body hitting the concrete.

"Poppy?" Jake pitched his voice low. "Where are you?"

In that moment, I forgave Jake for everything—every lie, every tear I'd cried over him, every patronizing comment. I rose up on my knees. "Here."

"We need to get out of here."

Duh.

"Who is that?" Thor demanded.

"Jake."

If we weren't in such danger, I would have said the sound coming from Thor was him grinding his teeth together.

"How many bad guys?" I whispered.

"Four."

There was still one out there.

"If we're ever in this situation again, don't warn me about a trap, Lead with the number of bad guys." I pulled one foot under me, ready to stand.

A gun pressed to the back of my neck put that idea on pause. We'd found our fourth bad guy. Or he'd found us.

"Come out, or princess here dies," said the man with the gun.

Jake didn't respond.

The man with the gun stood to my left. He hadn't bothered

to grab me. I still had full range of motion. As long as Jake didn't do anything idiotic like surrender, we had a chance.

"I'm counting to five, then she's nothing but scrambled brains on the floor. One. Two. Three—"

"Okay. Don't shoot her."

For an instant, Number Four's focus shifted from my neck to Jake.

I dropped all the way to the floor and kicked Number Four's legs out from under him.

Number Four fell backward and hit the floor with a sickening thud.

I scrabbled across the floor and pressed my gun against his head. "We're good, Jake."

"What the hell did you do?" Jake demanded.

"I knocked him down." Duh.

"You're sure there were just four?"

"They figured four would be more than enough to handle Poppy," Thor replied.

Number Four twitched.

I increased the pressure of the gun against his head. "Give me a reason." Not that I could shoot a man in cold blood, but Number Four didn't know that.

Jake turned on his phone's flashlight, nearly blinding me. "Stone, can you walk?"

Thor pushed himself off the floor and took a slow step. "Yeah?"

"What do we do with this guy?" I asked.

Jake hauled Number Four off the floor and kicked his gun halfway across the warehouse. "Who do you work for?"

Number Four shook his head.

"Mistake," Jake warned. "The lady wouldn't have shot you. I will. I'll ask again. Who do you work for?"

Apparently Number Four believed Jake's threat. He answered, "Vic Klein."

"Vic Klein is dead." I'd killed him.

"Doesn't mean his organization disappeared."

"Who's running it?" Jake demanded.

"Some guy."

"Some guy?" Sunny, laid-back Jake was a memory. The man who'd replaced him was frightening. That guy tapped the muzzle of his gun against Number Four's temple. "You can do better than that."

"She dies—" Number Four jerked his head in my direction "—and I get paid. That's all I know."

"The others? We should get out of here." Thor leaned—heavily—on an alligator head the size of a small house.

Jake pistol-whipped Number Four and grinned when the man crashed to the floor.

Thor tugged on my arm. "Let's go."

I resisted. "Wait. Did either of you hear where my lipstick landed?"

"Are you kidding me?" Jake looked as if he wouldn't mind holding his Glock to my head next.

He didn't understand. "It's the perfect shade and a limited edition and—" I turned on the flashlight on my phone "—I can't replace it and—" I clapped my hand over my mouth.

"What?" Jake demanded.

"Look." I pointed to the remains of the monkey whose shadow I'd used. Next to the destroyed simian lay the man in the yellow hat. "Just like Mama Vielle said."

Thor, who knew nothing about the spirits who'd whispered in Mama Vielle's ear, draped his arm around my shoulders. "I don't think we're finding your lipstick."

Thor's arm was dead weight. The man was barely standing.

"Fine. I'll get Chariss's PA to track down another one. We should go."

"Can you make it to the parking lot?" Jake had noticed how shaky Thor was.

"I'll be all right," Thor replied. "Everything feels numb after sitting for so long."

"I would have been here sooner, but someone kidnapped Rose."

"She's leaving out the part where someone tried to kidnap her too."

I shot Jake a dirty look and skirted a giant fleur-de-lis.

"Why set a trap for a woman you're going to kidnap?" asked Thor.

"Two groups of bad guys," I guessed. "Vic Klein's and somebody else's."

"Whose?"

"We can talk about that later. Right now, let's get you home."

We emerged from the warehouse and I paused and looked up at the sky. The night air felt soft on my skin and the river's song was pure music after the sound of gunshots.

"Good to be alive, huh?"

I smiled at Thor. "It is."

When we finally made it to the parking lot, Thor's brows rose. "You brought the Ferrari?"

"It was the only option."

"You'll have to sit on my lap, Poppy," Thor said.

"Like hell she will."

Three adults. Two of them large men. No backseat. "Okay, Jake. I'll drive, and you can sit on Mark's lap."

Jake's eyes narrowed. "You should have thought of this earlier."

Me? "You could have thought of it, but you were too busy telling me what a terrible driver I am."

"You obliterated a lawnmower!"

Thor limped over to the passenger seat and waited.

"And—" Jake jabbed his finger at me "—I can't believe the risks you took in that warehouse."

"What risks?"

"Shooting that lightbulb out! You gave away your position."

"Wait," said Thor. "Poppy shot out the lightbulb?"

Jake and I interrupted our staring (glaring) match and stared at him instead. "Yes."

Thor grinned. "Nice shooting."

"Thank you."

"Don't encourage her."

"Could you have made that shot?" Thor asked.

Jake shrugged. "Of course."

"Seriously?" Thor looked doubtful.

"Probably." A sliver of doubt was the only concession Jake would give.

I'd had enough. "Unlock the car, Jake."

Looking as if he'd rather eat glass, Jake unlocked the car.

Thor lowered himself into the passenger seat and I climbed onto his lap. "I'm not hurting you, am I?"

Jake snorted.

Thor grinned. Again. "Not at all. You're light as a feather. You feel great."

It was a good thing looks couldn't actually kill, or Jake's would've sent Thor to an early grave.

Thor smelled faintly of sweat and blood and gunpowder.

I breathed deeply. "I'm so glad you're okay."

"Can we talk strategy?" Jake ground out. "Please?"

"Tonight we rest," I declared.

"Sounds good to me," said Thor.

"Someone wants you dead, Poppy." Jake's hand gripped the gearshift so tightly his knuckles turned white.

"Seems as if someone always wants me dead." I leaned my head against Thor's shoulder.

"This is serious!" Jake hit the heel of his hand against the dashboard. Mr. Laid-Back was in a snit.

"I know, Jake. But we're tired. Tomorrow we'll track down John Howard. I'll call Lyman Cox about a tour of the port, and we'll see if René or Mr. Brown has any additional information about Billy Bouchet."

"Since when are you on a first-name basis with the detective?" Not just a snit—a major snit.

"Since he gave me my gun back?"

"Who's Billy Bouchet?" Thor asked.

"One of the guys who kidnapped Rose," I explained.

"He tried to kidnap Poppy." Jake downshifted, and the car roared.

"What happened?" asked Thor.

"He failed."

Thor chuckled. "That's my girl."

"She's. Not. Your. Girl."

This was turning into the longest short drive ever. I might as well add the cherry on top. "We've got a brunch tomorrow."

"A brunch?" Jake's voice was a blade.

I nodded. "At the Court of Two Sisters. It will only take a few hours."

"Priorities, Poppy."

"René's looking for Rose and I came here to be in Adele's wedding. This other stuff can wait." There was no way I'd be responsible for spoiling any part of Adele and Carter's celebration.

"Do you think the people trying to kill you will wait till after the wedding?" An epic snit.

"Lighten up, Jake. I'm going to that brunch."

"Fine. I'll take you."

"They think Mark is my boyfriend."

"Absolutely not."

"You don't get to make decisions for me."

He downshifted again and the engine roared.

"If you blow a rod in this car, you're having it repaired and you get to tell James what happened."

Jake shot a death glare my way.

It was a relief when we pulled into the courtyard and the gate swung shut behind us. I jumped out of the car.

Consuela and Ladybug waited for us.

"Thank heavens you're all right," Ladybug breathed.

"*Yip.*" You had me worried.

I scooped Consuela into my arms. She licked my nose.

I held her close. "I'm going to call Mama Vielle, then go to bed." I'd had enough of Jake for one night, but I glanced at Thor. "I promised Mama Vielle we'd go see her. Maybe we could stop by the hospital after brunch?"

Thor glanced at Jake and his eyes twinkled. "Sure."

"Great. I'll see you in the morning."

I left them, but not before I heard Jake say, "You and me, we have to talk."

Chapter Sixteen

I should have slept poorly. Tossed. Turned. There were so many things deserving of my worry. Where was Rose? Was John Howard crooked? Were the Arnauts mixed up in this mess—and what was Carter's big secret? Would Vic Klein's people make another attempt on my life? But I was exhausted. My head touched the pillow and I was out.

When I woke up, Consuela was curled on the pillow next to mine.

I stretched.

She yawned.

"Today will be a better day."

"*Yip*." Don't tempt fate.

I jammed my arms in a robe (baffled cotton that covered me from neck to knee) and went in search of coffee.

Chester was in the kitchen wiping a smudge off the front of the refrigerator door. He smiled when he saw me. "Good morning, Miss Fields. Coffee?"

"Please." I chose a stool at the granite island and sat.

Chester poured me a cup and put it and a small pitcher of cream in front of me.

"Thank you." I added cream, wrapped my hands around the mug, and drank. "Mmmm. Chester, you make a mean cup of coffee."

"What can I make you for breakfast?"

"Nothing, thank you. I'm having brunch at the Court of Two Sisters."

His face fell. "Surely you need a little something to tide you over?"

I didn't. Eating breakfast before brunch wasn't my thing. But Chester seemed so desperate to cook for someone, I couldn't say no. "A very little something. Do I have time for a shower?"

He rubbed his hands together. "Breakfast will be ready in thirty minutes."

I grabbed a quick shower, dried my hair, did my makeup, and donned the dress Lillian earmarked for brunch. No ruffles. No monograms. But definitely floral and bright.

When I returned to the kitchen, platters of French toast with caramelized bananas, crisp bacon and fat sausages, scrambled eggs, grits, blueberry muffins, and fresh-squeezed orange juice covered the island.

Jake and Thor sat on stools with fully loaded plates in front of them.

I refilled my coffee and helped myself to eggs and a slice of bacon.

Chester frowned. "You need to eat more than that, Miss Fields."

"Chester, if I ate half of this, I wouldn't fit into my bridesmaid's dress, and it's too late for major alterations."

"What does it look like?" asked Jake. "The dress?"

I closed my eyes and shuddered. "It's chiffon and there are ruffles. Have you ever seen me wear ruffles?"

"No."

"Or chiffon?"

"What's chiffon?"

"What color is it?" asked Thor.

"Lavender." Part of me believed Adele didn't realize how awful those ruffled lavender gowns were. Most of me believed she'd made absolutely sure no one outshined her on her wedding day. "Lavender," I repeated, just in case they missed the awfulness.

Thor didn't seem to grasp the gravity of lavender. He forked an enormous mouthful of eggs.

"You realize we're due at brunch in less than an hour, right?"

Thor stared at me as if he didn't see the problem with eating breakfast right before brunch. "No way it could be better than this."

Chester grinned. "Leave him alone, Miss Fields. I like seeing people eating my food. Most of the time, it's just me and Ladybug, and she eats like a bird."

"*Yip.*" Consuela would eat. Bacon, please.

I broke off a tiny piece and gave it to her.

She licked her doggy lips.

Jake took a sip of coffee. "While you two are at brunch, I'm going to track down John Howard."

"Are you sure that's a good idea?" I teased, adding a healthy dose of sugar to my tone.

Jake cocked his head. "Why wouldn't it be?"

"You'll be on your own. You won't have backup." My voice was sweeter still.

"So?"

"I'll worry."

Thor grinned.

Jake shook his head. "This is totally different."

By different, he meant he was a big, strong man and I was just a helpless female. "Oh?" The little arrow on my sugary voice meter was in the red zone.

Chester seemed to understand something was brewing. And he wanted no part of it. He wiped his hands on his apron. "If you don't need anything else, I'm gonna run a plate over to Miss Lenore."

"Who's Miss Lenore?" I asked—not a hint of sugar in my voice.

"The lady next door." Chester quickly filled a plate with eggs, bacon, a muffin, and a bowl of grits. "She's lived there longer than anyone can remember. Sometimes I take over food and visit a spell."

He hurried out the door with the plate for the neighbor.

I turned to Jake. "You were saying?"

"Just that I'm trained, and you're not."

"That'll soon be fixed."

Jake's face tightened. "We face down monsters. The things they do to women—I won't apologize for wanting to keep you far from people like that."

"But it's okay for you?"

"I'm gonna get ready for brunch." Thor backed out of the kitchen with his hands up. Like Chester, he wanted no part of this argument.

Jake pinched the bridge of his nose. "It's different for me."

"How?"

"It just is. I mean—look at you." He waved his free hand at me.

I glanced down at my dress—a floral Valentino. I didn't look tough—but how I looked wasn't the point. "I held my own yesterday."

"You had a gun pressed against the back of your skull yesterday."

A point I couldn't argue. "I don't see you worrying about Mark."

"I'm not in love with Mark." Jake's words hung in the air like a soap bubble.

We watched them hang there, bobbing above Chester's breakfast spread.

"*Yip.*" Did I remember the horrible lies Jake told me because he loved me?

Consuela made an excellent point. I rewarded her with another bite of bacon.

"Look, Poppy, I know I haven't always made the right choices when it comes to you, but—"

I held up my hand. Hearing about how Jake loved me was too painful. "Not now, Jake." Not ever. "Go investigate John Howard. Look into Lyman Cox. Who knows, maybe you can find Rose while Mark and I linger over a second cup of coffee."

"Poppy—"

"Your version of loving me makes me less than I am."

Jake didn't have a response for that. There wasn't one.

THOR and I walked the short distance to the Court of Two Sisters. No one followed us, which made for a nice change.

A maître d' led us to a brick courtyard with a burbling fountain, a wishing well, and lacy wrought-iron trellises covered with wisteria vines. A jazz trio played softly.

Four tables in a sun-dappled corner were covered with lavender linens. Bowls of white roses spilled petals and fragrance. Silverware gleamed.

"Pretty," Thor murmured.

"It is," I agreed as Patrice Coombs wrapped me in an enormous hug.

"You poor dear." She squeezed me tighter. "You've had the worst luck since you arrived in New Orleans. First that horrible tragedy at the Columns and now a near-kidnapping." She released me from her embrace and looked into my eyes. "I've lived here my whole life and never seen a bit of violence. When I saw you on the news last night, I nearly died."

Patrice's concern reminded me I hadn't called Chariss. If she learned about my latest brush with danger from *TMZ*, she'd be furious with me for a month, maybe two. My fingers itched to pick up the phone and at least text her. Instead, I smiled at Patrice. "I'd say my luck is pretty good. Those were two terrible situations and I'm fine."

"Glass half full. I like that." She glanced at Mark, who'd slipped away. He stood in line at a bar set up for the Coombs's guests.

A single wrinkle creased her forehead and she glanced down at the aged stones beneath our feet. "I hope you don't mind, but Knox Arnaut asked to be seated next to you."

"I don't mind at all."

"I think he was a little disappointed when Mark arrived. It's partly my fault, you see. I told everyone Adele's beautiful, glamorous friend was single—"

"Mark is new." Three days new. "There's no way you could have known."

She patted my hand. "Well, he's certainly handsome."

Thor was definitely handsome. I stared at him for a few long seconds. He wore khakis and a navy blazer and an Hermés tie the color of orange sherbet.

Patrice reclaimed my attention. "There's Carter's Great Aunt Agnes." She nodded toward a tiny woman whose eyeglasses were bigger than her head. Somehow the tortoiseshell frames worked for her. As did the flamingo pink dress paired with a vintage Chanel jacket and branch coral necklaces circling her thin neck. "Will you excuse me, please?"

"Of course."

Knox Arnaut immediately took Patrice's place at my side. "I saw you on the news."

"It must have been a slow news day."

"Oh, I don't know—a beautiful woman beating up a would-be kidnapper in the Vieux Carré is pretty much guaranteed to be the lead story around here." Knox took a sip from his mint-filled glass. "I reckon it'll be the lead story on the national news tonight."

Chariss would have kittens if I didn't call her. Soon.

"You know how to protect yourself." The tone of his voice made the ability to take care of myself sound like a sin. And, if his tone wasn't enough to put my back up, his accompanying smirk was.

"Just a few self-defense classes." I glanced around the patio. "Oh! Look! Adele and Carter are here. I'm going to say hello." I left him and his smirk standing there, hurried toward Adele, and kissed the air next to her perfectly made-up cheek.

"How are you feeling?" Her anxious gaze searched my face. "Did you get some rest?"

"I did. I'm fine."

"Poppy, may I get you a drink?" asked Carter.

"I think Mark's taking care of that." We all looked toward the bar where Mark chatted with the bartender.

"So he is. Adele, julep, bloody, or mimosa?"

"Mimosa."

Carter walked away and Adele leaned closer to me. "Jammies or sexy nightgown?"

"Jammies."

She wrinkled her nose. "What a waste."

Before I could think of a smart response, Thor handed me a mimosa.

I smiled up at him. "Thank you."

"You're welcome." Our gazes caught. And held.

"How are you finding New Orleans, Mark?" Adele asked.

"Beautiful and exciting."

She tittered. "Are you talking about the city or Poppy?"

Thor flushed and turned his gaze away. "Both."

Pete Coombs saved him from saying anything more by tapping a spoon against his glass. "Thank you for joining us this morning. This is the last Sunday my daughter will be known as Adele Coombs. Everyone, please raise your glasses. A toast to the lovely Adele Coombs, soon to be Adele Arnaut. We wish you all the happiness in the world, sugar."

Glass clinked and the Coombs's guests drank.

"Now, my wife has asked me to tell you the buffet is open."

Everyone milled for a moment, looking for their place cards so they knew where to leave their drinks. As Patrice had promised, I was seated next to Knox. What she hadn't told me was that Mark was at another table—the one with the single bridesmaids.

The buffet table was laden with turtle soup au sherry, shrimp Creole, eggs Benedict, crawfish pasta, shrimp étouffée, jambalaya, and veal grillades and gravy over grits. There were so many desserts—bananas Foster, pecan pie, King's cake, bread pudding with whiskey sauce, pralines, fruit pies, and cheesecake—they had their own table.

I took the seat next to Knox.

"I'm having a small cocktail party tonight," he said. "You and Matt are coming." A statement, not a question.

"Mark," I corrected. A cocktail party? Tonight? "I don't think it's on my calendar."

"Just an impromptu celebration," Knox continued. "No one

older than thirty allowed. It would mean so much to Adele if you came. She's worried your trip to New Orleans will leave you permanently scarred."

I did not need another party.

"I tried calling you last night, but you didn't answer your phone. All the other bridesmaids will be there."

What could I say? "We wouldn't miss it." Jake's head was going to pop off his neck.

We spent the rest of the meal talking about the Saints and the Pelicans—I hadn't realized New Orleans had an NBA team. Knox found my ignorance hilarious.

"Poppy—"

I looked up at Mark.

"If we're going to stop by the hospital, we should probably go."

Knox frowned at the interruption to his Saints-were-robbed-in-the-NFC-championship story. "Who's in the hospital?"

I swallowed my annoyance—the less Knox Arnaut knew about my life the better. "Mama Vielle."

"The voodoo woman who told your fortune?" His frown deepened. "Why are you visiting her?"

"Because she asked me to." I laid my napkin on the table and stood. "Knox, so nice talking to you."

"What took you so long?" I whispered to Thor as we walked away.

"It took me that long to break away." He looked back at his table.

Four pretty young women simpered and waved.

"Let's say thank you to Pete and Patrice, then we can go."

Moments later, we climbed into the backseat of the Uber Thor ordered.

I pulled out my phone and texted Chariss. Little hiccup yesterday. You may see video. I am fine. No cause for alarm.

It was too little, too late, and I knew it.

"Can you take us to a florist?" I asked the driver.

He nodded.

When we arrived at the hospital, I held a vase filled with delphiniums and Thor had a box of chocolates tucked under his arm. We found Mama Vielle's room and I raised my hand to knock.

"Poppy, wait." A flush darkened Thor's cheeks. "We haven't had a moment alone since the warehouse. You came for me."

"You'd have done the same for me."

"Thank you."

"You're welcome." I lifted my hand again.

"I hope coming after me won't hurt your relationship with Smith."

My relationship with Jake? "No. What was between us is over. Whether or not we can remain friends is to be decided."

An unreadable expression flashed across Thor's face and he pulled on his tie. "Look, getting involved again is probably the last thing you want, but—"

"It is." My voice was too loud.

His face fell.

"I mean—" I swallowed "—it's too soon." The electric current that often sparked between Thor and me was undeniable, but I wasn't ready. "Our timing is off."

"The only problem is timing?"

I nodded.

"Timing can change."

"It can," I agreed.

"I'm not going anywhere."

Good to know. I hid a smile and knocked on Mama Vielle's door.

"Come in."

Mama Vielle looked smaller without her gauzy black clothes and heavy beads. And she looked tired.

I carried the flowers to the window sill and put them down. "Mama Vielle, this is my friend Mark Stone."

He held out the chocolates. "It's nice to meet you. Thank you for saving Poppy."

She took the box. "Lord, but you're a fine-looking man. Sit."

Thor smiled and sat in the chair next to the bed.

"The spirits been whispering to me," she told him.

"Oh?" Thor sounded scrupulously polite.

"What did the spirits say?" I asked. The man in the yellow hat had made me a believer.

"Just one word, and I didn't understand it."

"What's the word?"

Mama Vielle picked at her blanket. "There's all sorts of darkness surrounding the spirits' word. It's dangerous. Best thing you could do is stay far away."

"What's the word?" I asked again.

"Venti."

Thor stared at the old woman in the bed. "Venti?"

Mama Vielle nodded.

"Where did you hear about Venti?"

"I told you. The spirits." A stubborn expression settled on Mama Vielle's face—she didn't appreciate his doubts.

But really, that spirits told Mama Vielle about Venti was only slightly less probable than the alternative—that the septuagenarian in the hospital bed was somehow involved in smuggling.

Thor patted his blazer, fished out his phone, and looked at

the screen. "I've got to take this." He nodded at Mama Vielle, stood, and walked into the hallway.

Mama Vielle followed him with her eyes. "He doesn't believe me."

"He didn't hear you talk about the man in the yellow hat."

"Hmmph." Her gaze settled on me. "Let me see your palm."

I settled into Thor's empty chair and held out my hand.

Mama Vielle perched a pair of glasses on her nose, took my hand in hers, and studied the lines on my skin. "You be careful. You run when you should walk and walk when you should run."

What the heck did that mean? "Do you see anything about Venti?"

"No."

"Poppy—" Thor stuck his head into the room "—I'm sorry to interrupt, but we need to go."

"We do?"

He nodded. "Mr. Brown called."

Gently, I tugged my hand loose of Mama Vielle's hold and stood. "We've got to go, but I'll come see you again."

She cackled. "You're gonna be too busy to come back to the hospital. And I don't plan on staying here much longer. You come see me at my house before you leave New Orleans."

"I will. I promise." I followed Thor into the hall. "What's happened?" It had to be bad.

"The police found Mason Hubbard's body."

Chapter Seventeen

"How well do you know that police detective?" Thor asked.

"Well enough to know he won't appreciate us poking around his investigation. Wait. Is René the lead investigator?" I stepped out of the elevator and into the hospital lobby.

Thor shook his head. "No."

"Did Mr. Brown say how Mason Hubbard died?"

"Someone cut off his head."

That stopped me in my tracks. "While he was alive?" My stomach flipped.

"I don't think they know yet." Thor took my elbow and pulled me out of the way of a man in a wheelchair with a devilish gleam in his eye. "You know who cuts off heads, right?"

"The Sinaloans." Drug cartels were vicious.

Thor nodded and we walked through the glass doors leading to the street.

I took a deep breath of humid air. "So, if Vic Klein was working for the Sinaloans, then it was probably his people who killed Mason." The same people who'd used Thor as bait. "What happened yesterday? How did they take you?"

"I don't know. I was walking toward Jackson Square when someone bumped into me. The next thing I remember is waking up in that warehouse."

"So they drugged you?"

"Yeah."

"I'm glad we got you out of there." Huge understatement.

"Me too."

I rubbed my forehead. "Who did Mason work for?"

"I called Mr. Brown and asked about that. According to him, Hubbard worked part-time at the port, saw some odd things going on, and reported them."

"Do you think he knew where the containers of Venti are?"

"Probably."

"Do you think he told the people who killed him?"

"Yeah."

"So someone will be moving those containers. Soon."

"Assuming he told them the truth."

"Does Mr. Brown have any idea who the other player is?"

"No." Thor looked left, then right. "There are no cabs."

"Can you get an Uber?"

"Yeah." He pulled out his cell and looked down at the screen.

I looked at the street in front of us. An older woman with a walker had pushed the crossing button and was shuffling across the street. The flashing crosswalk signs had drivers slowing down—except for a black Escalade barreling toward us.

"Mark!"

He looked up from his phone.

"Get down!"

We hit the banquette as gunfire erupted from the SUV—sprayed from the SUV. There were bullets everywhere.

And screams.

And the shattering of the hospital's glass doors.

The Escalade raced away. Mark pushed off the pavement and ran after it.

It was official—I was *over* black SUVs.

He ran for a block—until the Escalade turned onto another street and disappeared.

I ran after him. "Did you get a plate?"

"The plates were probably stolen."

Behind us, people cried. A man threw up. A woman hyperventilated.

But no one bled.

"I really hate being shot at."

Thor nodded. "Me too."

"How did they find us?"

Thor took out his phone—the phone he'd been astonished to find in his pocket when we left the warehouse—dropped it on the pavement, and crushed the casing under his heel.

I stared down at the destroyed phone.

"I should have realized. I nearly got you killed. I'm sorry."

"Sorry?"

"If you hadn't been paying attention—"

"Don't go getting protective."

"I'm not. I'd apologize to any partner."

"We're fine."

"Thanks to you."

My phone rang, and I glanced down at the screen then answered. "Detective Langlois, are you psychic?"

"No. Why?" His voice held a sharp edge.

Thor drew his finger across his throat and shook his head.

"Um...I was just thinking of you and you called. What can I do for you?"

"Do you own an enameled lipstick case? Black with a gold monogram?"

"I do. James had it made for me—" Too late I remembered where I'd last had that lipstick case. "Did you find it?"

"When did you last see it?" Definitely a sharp edge, but laced with exhaustion. I could picture him at his desk. One hand pressing the receiver to his ear. The other pinching the bridge of his nose.

"Yesterday."

"Yesterday?"

I thought quick. "I used the lipstick right before the altercation with Billy Bouchet." Not strictly a lie. Definitely not the whole truth.

"Any idea why it would show up at a warehouse by the river?"

Oh, dear. "No. No idea. Was the lipstick still inside the case?"

"The lipstick?"

"It's my favorite and Sisley discontinued the color and—"

"I don't know if there's still a lipstick inside, Miss Fields."

"Would you check?"

If I hadn't pegged René Langlois as a laid-back guy, I'd have guessed the sound coming through the phone was him grinding his teeth together.

Time for a new subject. "Have you had any luck looking for Rose?"

"No." Just one word, but it gave me the impression he wasn't telling me the whole truth either.

The sound of approaching sirens reached us.

"Is there anything else, Detective?"

"Miss Fields." The edge returned to his voice. With a vengeance. "Where are you?"

"Just standing on the banquette."

"I hear sirens."

"It's a city. There are sirens."

"Not that many. Where are you?"

"Detective? It's getting awfully loud here. I can barely hear you. I'll call you later." I hung up and said to Thor, "We should probably go."

He nodded and we hurried down the banquette, putting as much distance between us and the hospital as possible.

"I could call Jake," I said.

Thor's brows rose.

"To come get us?"

"The Ferrari again?"

"He could borrow Ladybug's car."

"Just get an Uber."

"I don't have the app."

His brows rose higher. "Then call a cab."

"What?"

"Use your phone and call." He mimed pushing buttons and holding a phone to his ear. "People used to do it all the time."

"No one likes a smartass."

Thor merely smiled.

The taxi picked us up a few blocks from the hospital.

When we'd settled into the backseat, I asked, "What next?"

"We check in with Jake, and I get a new phone."

"How about we reverse the order?" I wasn't exactly excited to tell Jake about the drive-by shooting or Knox Arnaut's cocktail party.

Forty-five minutes and one new phone later, we arrived at James's house. Jake wasn't there.

I picked up Consuela and held her close. "We've got about a couple of hours till we're due at Knox's cocktail party."

"What?" Thor winced. "That's not on the calendar."

"*Yip.*" The party wasn't on Consuela's calendar either.

"I know. I'm sorry. But he wouldn't take no for an answer."

"There's something off about that guy."

"*Yip.*" Consuela agreed.

"I don't see how I can get out of going. He's Carter's cousin. We don't have to stay long."

"What do we have tomorrow?"

"You have nothing. I have a spa day."

"A spa day?"

"Massage. Facial. Mani/pedi. Afterward, we're going to the Carousel Bar for drinks. On Tuesday, I've got a final fitting for the dress, then we're all having lunch at Commander's Palace. Adele said something about twenty-five cent martinis. Then parties Wednesday and Thursday nights, the rehearsal on Friday followed by dinner, a brunch on Saturday, the wedding, and another brunch on Sunday."

Thor blinked.

I stretched. "I'm going to change my dress and fix my makeup."

An hour later, Jake still wasn't home.

I found Thor in the screening room, watching the news—a reporter stood in front of the hospital's shattered doors. "I'm worried," I said.

"They're reporting the shooting was random."

"I'm worried about Jake."

"He can take care of himself."

"That's what he said about you before I found you tied to a chair in a warehouse. If Jake would answer his phone or text me back, I'd feel better."

"What do you want to do, Poppy?"

"I don't know."

"I can track him down and meet you at Arnaut's later."

"You'd do that?"

"You didn't come to that warehouse by yourself."

Thor drove me to Knox's apartment building in the Warehouse District. I rode the elevator to the penthouse floor alone and rang the bell.

Knox opened the door. "Poppy!" He peered past me. "No boyfriend?"

"He had a business call."

"On a Sunday night?"

"It's not Sunday night in Hong Kong." Or maybe it was. Keeping track of time zones wasn't one of my strong points. "But I did bring a date."

Consuela poked her head out of my handbag. "*Grrrr.*"

"Wow. She's adorable."

"*Grrrr.*"

Knox beckoned me inside. The best thing about his home was the view of the river. Aside from that, his apartment could have been in New York with a view of the Hudson, or San Francisco with a view of the bay. There was nothing in the whole place—not one thing—that suggested New Orleans.

"Do you like it?" he asked.

I scanned the modern furniture and the modern art. "The view is phenomenal."

"It is, isn't it? How was Mama Vielle?"

It hit me—Thor's phone wasn't the only way the shooters could have tracked us to the hospital. Knox knew exactly where we were going. Was he mixed up in all this? I swallowed and found my voice. "She's feeling stronger."

"You didn't explain why you were visiting her."

"Yes, I did. I went because she asked me to come."

"How do you know her?" he insisted.

"You introduced us."

"Yes, but—"

"There you are!" Adele grabbed my arm. "Just the person I've been looking for! You'll let me steal her away, won't you, Knox?"

"If you bring her back." Knox's smile was strained.

Adele whooshed me out onto the balcony. "Are you all right? For a second there you looked as if you might faint." She glanced over her shoulder. "Where's Mark?"

"Work call. He'll be here later." I didn't like lying to Adele, but I could hardly tell her my pretend boyfriend was out searching for my ex-boyfriend.

"*Yip.*" I wasn't to worry, they'd both be okay.

"You brought Consuela! You have to introduce her to the girls! They'll love her."

"*Yip.*" Of course they would.

I followed Adele to the cluster of bridesmaids. They were all from New Orleans, had all known each other since birth, and all thought I'd be more fun than I actually was. Oh, and they all thought Thor was gorgeous.

"Isn't she just the cutest thing ever?" said Laura. "May I pet her?"

"Let her sniff your hand first."

Laura held out her hand and Consuela sniffed. "*Yip.*" Laura was worthy of the honor of petting her.

Consuela went so far as to let Laura scratch behind her ears.

"Is she a therapy dog?"

"No."

"You should totally get her certified—then you could take her everywhere."

"*Yip.*" What a great idea.

"How long have you and Mark been together?" asked another bridesmaid—Katie. She glanced down at the river, not quite hiding the acquisitive expression in her eyes.

An emotion I didn't care to identify lifted its head, sniffed the air, and bared its teeth. Thor was mine—or he would be—

someday—maybe. Regardless, Katie better keep her paws off him. "Not long."

She cast her gaze around Knox's soulless apartment until she found our host. "I know a man who'd like to take his place."

These were Adele's friends—I could be nice. I forced a smile. "Why is Knox still single? It seems as if some girl should have talked him out of a ring by now."

"Knox's last girlfriend..." Katie bit her lip and returned her gaze to the river.

"What?"

"He likes it rough," Laura supplied.

Too much information. It was time for another subject. "How does he afford all this?"

"His daddy must be helping out," said Laura. "No way does a deputy district attorney make enough to live here."

"Knox has a trust." Katie brought her gaze back to our little circle. "The trust pays for this place."

"Where'd you hear that?" asked Laura.

"His last girlfriend, Anne-Marie, is friends with my older sister."

"Anne-Marie Landry told you that?" Laura's disbelief was apparent.

"No. She told my sister. My sister told me."

Adele, whose manners were too refined to allow her to gossip about her host, changed the subject. "What's everyone having done tomorrow?"

Two hours passed. I sipped cocktails. I nibbled on grilled shrimp. I heard all about a Mississippi mud wrap and decided I'd sooner die. Thor didn't come.

Nor did he answer his texts. All fifteen of them.

He'd joined Jake among the missing.

"*Yip.*" Consuela was worried too.

With a knot of dread in my stomach, I found my host. "Knox, thank you for a lovely evening, but—"

"You can't leave."

"I'm exhausted and we have a big day tomorrow."

He narrowed his eyes. "Isn't tomorrow the spa day?"

"It is, and I don't want to fall asleep on the massage table."

"We haven't had a chance to talk."

"Another time? I really should go." I took out my phone.

"What are you doing?"

"Calling a cab."

"A cab?" He waved off the idea. "I'll take you home."

"You're hosting a party."

"Adele and Carter and their friends will be fine without me. It'll only take me a few minutes to run you home."

How did he know that? "You know where I'm staying?"

Knox blinked. "Someone must have mentioned it. As for taking you home, I insist."

I'd side-stepped pushier men than Knox Arnaut—but none of those men were related (about-to-be-related) to one of my best friends. I ceded, "Let me tell Adele I'm leaving."

"You needn't bother—"

"I couldn't possibly leave without saying good bye." Especially since I wasn't sure if Knox tipped someone off about Thor's and my trip to the hospital. I left him standing next to the bar.

Adele, when I found her, was deep in conversation with Carter.

"Sorry to interrupt."

"You're not interrupting." Carter might well have been the most polite man on the planet.

"I just wanted to say good night. Knox is running me home."

"Knox?" Adele's eyes searched the living room. "Where's

Mark?"

"His call must have taken longer than he counted on." We hadn't added tracking to Thor's new phone. How was I going to find him? The dread in my stomach was growing tentacles.

"I'll take you home, Poppy," Carter offered.

"Thank you, but I don't want to—"

"I should take you home. My cousin—"

"No need to leave your fiancée, Carter." Knox stood next to us. "I'll take Poppy home."

The two men stared at each other for a moment—some kind of pissing contest I didn't understand—then Carter looked away.

Adele's nervous laugh didn't make things any better. "I'll see you in the morning. Ten o'clock?"

I air-kissed her cheek. "I'll be there."

"Knox, you drive safely. And Poppy, be safe."

"*Yip.*" Consuela would protect me.

Consuela and I rode the elevator to the building's garage with Knox, then followed him to a black Audi R8.

"Nice car."

Knox stroked the roof and opened the passenger door for me. "Thank you."

He circled to the driver's side, slipped behind the wheel, and grinned at me. "Ready?"

"Yes."

Knox peeled out of the parking lot.

I held onto Consuela. Tightly.

"*Grrr.*" Consuela wasn't wearing a seatbelt and didn't appreciate Knox's driving. Not one bit.

"Where do you live in California?" he asked.

I tightened my grip on Consuela. "Malibu."

"On the beach?"

"Yes."

He swerved around a slow-moving Honda. "Must be nice."

"It is, but it doesn't have New Orleans' sense of history."

He wrinkled his nose. "That's overrated."

"I don't know about that. Waiters might recognize me, but they don't know me. Not like Charles knows you. No one has deep roots."

"No one has expectations of you based on your grandfather or your great-grandfather. Sounds good to me."

My foot pressed against a phantom brake pedal. "Maybe not my grandfather. But when you're a star's kid, there are definitely expectations."

He snorted softly. Any issues I faced were nothing to his challenges.

Given that we'd just left his million-dollar apartment and were speeding down Decatur in a car that could make James Ballester drool, I didn't have much sympathy.

Knox turned left—fast enough to fishtail—then left again, and came to a screeching stop in front of James' house.

I opened the car door. "Thank you for the ride."

"You're not going to ask me in?"

"*Grrrr.*"

"You're still hosting a party." I got out and closed the door.

For a second, I thought Knox would leave the car double-parked and walk me to the door. Instead, he rolled down his window. "Don't let the old-world charm fool you, Poppy. New Orleans is a dangerous place."

As if I needed reminding. "Thanks again. Good night." I hurried inside and called, "Mark? Jake?"

Ladybug appeared at the top of the stairs. "They haven't come home yet."

I put Consuela down and walked into the living room. "What should I do?"

Neither Consuela nor the ghost answered.

I didn't have the first idea where to look for them. Something was wrong. Terribly wrong. I was sure of it.

I sank onto the couch and pulled my phone out of my purse. I stared at the ceiling for long seconds. Finally, I dialed.

"What is it, Miss Fields?" Mr. Brown's voice was flat.

"Jake and Mark are missing."

"Missing?"

"They're not here."

"Here being?"

"Home. I think they're in trouble."

"Based on?"

"Mark was supposed to meet me at a party and he didn't show up."

Mr. Brown let his silence speak for him. He didn't have a crystal ball. He couldn't tell me where they were. What I did next was up to me, but I was being needlessly dramatic.

"What if—"

"Miss Fields—"

"Jake didn't come back this afternoon and Mark went to look for him and now they're both gone." I spoke so quickly the words tripped over each other.

Mr. Brown replied with more silence.

"There are Sinaloans here. And that federal agent, John Howard—the one who was there when men opened fire on the Columns—who knows what he's up to. And Lyman Cox—he gives me the heebie jeebies. And Knox—" I stopped myself. The one place I was sure they weren't was with Knox Arnaut.

"I'm hanging up now, Miss Fields. If I hear anything, I'll call."

I texted both Thor and Jake.

Neither one answered.

Feeling completely helpless, I curled up on the couch to wait.

Chapter Eighteen

"Miss Fields?"

I opened my eyes to sunlight filtering through the living room curtains. A beam touched Consuela, who was curled at the end of the sofa, turning her tawny fur into spun gold. She yawned like the princess she was.

Ladybug stood in the doorway with a worried expression on her face.

I rubbed the back of my neck. I'd fallen asleep in the corner of the couch, waiting for men who didn't come home, and now a crick shot pain into my skull and spine. "Are they back?" Hope sparked in my chest.

"No."

The little spark guttered, and I swung my feet to the floor and reached for my phone. Maybe one of them had texted.

The only text I'd received was from Adele: Call me when you get up.

Had I missed a call? I scrolled. "Ladybug, may I have some coffee, please?"

"Of course, but—"

I glanced up at her.

"There's someone here to see you."

"Who?"

"He says his name is John Howard."

Everything stilled—my finger on the cell screen, time, my heart. "You're sure that's his name?"

"Yes."

"Where is he?"

"I asked him to wait in the front hall."

John Howard. Jake's plan for yesterday included investigating John Howard. Now Jake was missing. And John Howard was here. What did he want? I swallowed. "Show him in."

Ladybug rubbed the tip of her nose. "You might want to—" She smoothed the fabric of her dress over her hips.

Oops. My dress had ridden up. Way up. And moss grew on my teeth. And my mascara had probably migrated to my chin. "Maybe I should clean up a bit."

She pursed her lips. "That might be for the best."

I hurried to my room, washed my face, and brushed my teeth and hair. I needed makeup—there were dark smudges beneath my eyes that had nothing to do with last night's mascara—but didn't take the time. Instead, I slipped into black pants, a tee-shirt, and my trusty Tod's loafers.

"*Yip.*" Don't forget your gun.

"Good idea." I changed out the tee-shirt for a loose cotton sweater and hid the gun against the small of my back. Then, with Consuela trotting beside me, I returned to the living room.

John Howard stood when I stopped in the doorway to the living room—a man with good manners. He looked exactly as he had when I first saw him a few days ago at the Columns—six feet tall, dark hair, brown eyes, divot in his chin—but this morning he wasn't carrying a weapon. At least not one I could see.

The gun pressing against my back gave me confidence. I crossed the threshold.

Ladybug had left a coffeepot, cups, and saucers on the table in front of the couch. I sat and poured myself a cup without saying a word. I needed caffeine and I couldn't think of a single thing to say except *what the hell are you doing here*? A valid question, but a rude way to start a conversation.

"You're probably wondering what the hell I'm doing here."

I swallowed a smile—a tiny, worried smile. "The thought crossed my mind."

Amusement flitted across his face. "Mine too."

"So why are you here?"

"Your boss sent me."

"My boss?"

Now he scowled. "Mr. Brown."

I sank back into the couch's down cushions. "Mr. Brown sent you? Here?"

"Apparently, you convinced him Smith was in trouble."

Smith, but not Stone? What was going on?

John Howard's scowl deepened, scoring deep lines from the edge of his nose to the edge of his lips. "He thought you might help find him."

"Me?"

"He said what you lacked in skills, you made up for in luck." That sounded exactly like Mr. Brown. "And that I was to include you in whatever I did." The flinty expression in John Howard's eyes said he wasn't happy about that.

"What are you going to do?"

He rubbed the pads of his fingers against his temples. "I talked to your boyfriend, Jake, yesterday."

Of course Jake would say he was my boyfriend. My fingers tightened around the cup's delicate handle. "Where is he?"

"I was hoping you'd heard from him."

"No, I haven't." I clasped my hands in my lap—mainly to keep them from shaking. "When did you seem him?"

"He left me around two."

And he'd been missing ever since. "What's going on, Mr. Howard?"

"John. You might as well call me John." He took a sip of coffee and stared at one of James's paintings.

I waited for an answer. And waited.

Finally, he shifted his gaze to me. "It's hard to know where to start. I've been undercover for two years. When you saw me at the Columns—"

My cup rattled in its saucer.

"Yes, I know you saw me at the Columns. Jake told me." He ran a hand over his chin. "There are things you may not understand about being undercover."

"Undoubtedly." I washed down the sarcasm in my tone with a large sip of coffee.

"There was nothing I could do about those people at the Columns."

"An innocent man died."

John lowered his head. "I know. I tried to stop the shooting. I ran up the stairs onto that veranda as fast as I could."

Surely he realized how flimsy that sounded. He'd obviously been the leader. Why had he allowed the men to open fire? But the tragedy at the Columns could be dealt with later. Right now, I cared about Jake. And Mark. Were they not together?

"Who are you investigating?"

"I was investigating corruption at the port, then Vic Klein arrived in town."

"What does a Sinaloan drug smuggler have to do with corruption?"

John's eyes narrowed and he rubbed his chin. "What do you know about drug smuggling?"

"About the actual movement of product from point A to point B? Not much. But I do know a lot about the Sinaloan cartel." An understatement. I took another needed sip of coffee and thought. Hard. "Vic Klein planned on moving massive quantities of Venti through the Port of New Orleans. He would have had to pay off a ton of people." I looked to John for confirmation. At his nod, I continued, "But something went wrong." I guessed. Wildly. "The person you're investigating decided to keep the payoff and the drugs."

John didn't react. Much. Only the thinning of his lips told me I was right.

My coffee cup was empty. I put it down on the table and refilled it. A few more caffeine-fueled guesses and I'd have the whole thing solved. "I'm guessing Lyman Cox."

"*Yip, yip, yip.*" You're right. You're totally right. And I don't like this guy.

"Assuming I'm right, it was Cox who told you to kill Klein."

"I didn't kill Klein. I wanted him alive. You killed him."

As if I needed reminding. "So, what's Cox's problem? The payoff was made. Klein is dead. He has the drugs."

John's mouth formed a blade-thin line.

"Cox doesn't have the drugs?" No wonder people were getting abducted and shot and buildings were blowing up. "Why not? Wait—" I held up my hand. The answer was obvious. "Mason Hubbard."

"Hubbard made the containers disappear."

"Disappear? Aren't they twenty feet long? How can someone just make a shipping container disappear?"

The corner of John's left eye twitched. "He didn't actually

make them disappear. He changed the tracking numbers in the system. The containers we thought held Venti are full of Cholula hot sauce."

A small, slightly hysterical giggle escaped me. Hot sauce? "Hubbard is dead. How will anyone ever find the right containers?" I took another wild guess. "Unless Hubbard told the people who killed him. The Sinaloans killed him?"

"It wasn't us."

"What about Rose O'Leary?"

He flushed. "We have her."

"And by we, you mean...?"

His cheeks colored slightly. "Me. I've got her stashed. For her safety."

That was a relief. Maybe. "You're behind the kidnapping?"

"It was the only way to keep her safe."

"Seems to me there were lots of ways to keep Rose safe without drugging her drink."

"You don't know what these people are capable of."

Well, that sounded needlessly ominous. And wrong. I knew exactly what drug cartels were capable of. And, if Lyman Cox had asked me, I'd have told him not to double cross the Sinaloans. "Do you think Jake is at the port?"

He shook his head. Either he didn't know, or he didn't want to tell me.

"I think he's at the port. Maybe we should go find him?" Like, now.

"*Grrr.*" You're not seriously thinking of going somewhere with this man?

Consuela brought up an excellent point. There were still plenty of holes in John Howard's story. But what choice did I have? The alternative was losing my mind with worry.

"Do you have a dress that will stop traffic?"

"Dozens of them."

He looked up at the ceiling. He looked down at his hands in his lap. He looked at me. Then he sighed. "Lyman Cox likes red."

"Give me thirty minutes."

Of course I called Mr. Brown. I stood in the bathroom with an array of makeup spread on the counter in front of me and let the phone ring.

"Hello, Miss Fields."

"Did you send John Howard?"

"I did."

My spine softened from steel rod to regular bone. "He doesn't seem very happy to be here."

"He's about to blow a two-year cover."

I rubbed tinted moisturizer into my skin. "Do you trust him?"

"Do you?"

My answer was immediate. "No."

"You have your answer."

"Then why—"

"Smith checked in with me at two o'clock yesterday. I haven't been able to reach him since. I can't reach Stone. I need someone to find them. Howard can get you in. Just watch your back."

That second cup of coffee had been a mistake—my stomach felt awash in acid. "Where was Jake when you talked to him?"

"His phone pinged off a tower near the port."

I swept blush across the apples of my cheeks and gripped the edge of the counter. "And Mark?"

"The last signal came from a tower near a hospital. You were with him."

And we hadn't thought to update Mr. Brown with Thor's new phone.

"About that—"

"Later. Right now I need you to find them."

Mr. Brown trusted me—maybe not my judgment or my skills—but at least he knew I wouldn't betray him. I picked up my favorite eyebrow pencil. "Is there anyone besides John Howard who could go with me?"

"If there were, they'd be at your house right now."

"What about the police detective?"

"What about him?"

Using feather strokes, I enhanced my left brow. "I trust him."

Mr. Brown didn't respond.

I filled in my right brow, curled my eyelashes, and pulled the wand out of the mascara.

"Do what you think is best."

Wow. Not what I was expecting. Mr. Brown had to be really worried.

"I'll have more people—my people—on the ground in a few hours, but—"

"But Jake and Mark may not have that long."

"Understand, Miss Fields—" his voice was grim "—you're taking an enormous risk."

What else could I do? I had to go. A man I'd once loved and my partner were in danger. It wasn't as if I could go to Adele's spa party and request an extra-long massage. "I understand. I'll keep you updated."

"Miss Fields—"

"Yes?"

"Try not to get yourself killed."

"I'll do my best." I hung up and dialed Adele's number. Relief swept through me when the call went to voicemail. "Adele, it's me—Poppy. Something's up with Mark and I won't be able to make it today. I'm sorry. Hope you all have a wonderful time."

I hung up, coated my lashes with mascara, then applied lipstick. I'd made myself up to look exactly like Chariss. Hopefully Lyman Cox was a fan.

I slipped into a red pencil skirt and clingy white top. I slid the gun into the waistband and covered it with a jacket. Then I glanced down at my feet. Sadly, the Tod's loafers wouldn't stop traffic. With a sigh, I slipped on a pair of leopard-print Blahniks.

"*Yip*." Consuela approved of the outfit.

"Thank you." I went to Thor's room, opened every drawer, felt between the box springs and the mattress, and checked his empty suitcase. I didn't find a single gun.

Next I went to Jake's room where I opened his underwear drawer and found a Glock nestled in his boxers. The clips were with his socks.

I took the gun and the ammunition, then called Detective Langlois. "René, this is Poppy Fields calling."

"Miss Fields, it's Monday morning, a new week—what say you avoid all shootings, kidnappings, and bombings?"

Too late for that. I swallowed. "You really ought to call me Poppy."

"How can I help you today, Poppy?" I winced at the wariness in his voice.

"Those things I can't tell you?"

"Yes?" I had his interest now.

"I still can't tell you, but I'd feel better if you were tracking my phone."

His long, drawn-out, shoulders-slumping, overworked sigh reminded me I'd made his life difficult since my arrival. "Where are you going?"

"The port."

"Which port?"

"There's more than one?"

"There's a terminal for cruise ships and—"

"Not there. I'm going wherever the international containers arrive."

Detective Langlois did not reply.

"Please, René? I'd tell you if I could."

"Miss Fields, I'll track your phone, but it would be better, for both of us, if you'd level with me."

"I wish I could." I really did. "I'm sorry." I really was. "I've got to go." I hung up and switched the phone to vibrate. Then I returned to my room, put Jake's gun, the spare clips, and a lipstick in my purse, and stared at the woman in the mirror. "You got this."

Neither one of us believed me.

I returned to the living room with five minutes to spare.

John Howard turned away from his study of James's bookshelves. "You look amazing."

"Thank you."

His gaze shifted to my feet. "I've found a parking spot on the street about a half-block from here. You won't have to walk far."

Thump!

I circled the couch and looked down at the ghost's latest message. *Invitation to a Beheading.* Oh, dear. I picked up the book and showed the cover to John. "I had no idea James read Nabokov." My voice didn't shake. Not a bit.

John looked from the shelf to the floor. "The book just fell. By itself."

"The resident ghost." I slipped the volume back into its place. "I'll follow you in my car."

John's face darkened. "I'll drive. We can go over the plan on the way."

"I thought the plan was for me to seduce Lyman Cox and get him to tell me where Jake is."

"There's more to the plan than that."

"Oh? What?"

"What about the containers?"

"With Mason Hubbard dead, that ship has sailed." A little port humor.

John was unamused. He strode halfway across the room, then turned and glared at me. "So you're going to seduce a man you don't know to rescue your boyfriend?"

Ex-boyfriend. "It was your idea."

"You seem so...sanguine."

"Big word for a federal agent."

"I went to Harvard before I joined the agency."

"Well, I grew up in Hollywood—" a town where sex was a commodity "—so a little seduction doesn't bother me."

That, and I had no intention of letting Lyman Cox lay a single finger on me.

Driving James's Ferrari, I followed John's Mercedes coupe down Royal Street onto Canal, then west.

Were Jake and Mark okay?

Were they together or in separate messes?

Where were the containers?

Was René tracking my phone? Would he send help if something happened to the signal?

All those questions disappeared when I saw the port—a city of cargo containers stacked five and six containers high and four or five abreast. There were bright blues and yellows and rust reds with the occasional pop of turquoise. The stacks stretched as far as the eye could see.

My foot eased off the gas pedal and parked the car. Was that—

I fumbled for my phone and dialed René.

"Who are you seeing at the port, Poppy?"

"Lyman Cox. But that's not why I called." I glanced at John's Mercedes. "Is there any reason—"

"Lyman Cox? At the port?"

"Yes."

"Why would Lyman Cox be at the actual port?"

My blood chilled. "What do you mean?"

"His office is on Canal Street."

That was bad. I had another question. "Why would Knox Arnaut be here?"

"I don't know."

Tap, tap.

I looked out the window at the muzzle of a gun.

Chapter Nineteen

"Detective, there's a man with a gun at my window."

"What?" René barked. "Who?"

"A federal agent named John Howard. He may—or may not—be dirty." I smiled up at John—brightly, lots of teeth. "At this moment, I'm leaning toward dirty."

Tap, tap. The tap coupled with a scowl told me John didn't appreciate waiting.

"Poppy, drive away," said René. "Now."

That was the smart thing to do. I knew it. Instead, I held up the phone, mouthed *just a minute,* and raised my hand for John to wait.

Tap, tap.

"He's not taking no for an answer." I rolled down the window but spoke into the phone, "Adele, I'm so sorry. I really am. I've got to go. Talk to you later." I hung up on a splorting Detective Langlois. "What's with the gun, John?"

He looked down at his hand as if he were surprised to find a Ruger grasped in his fingers, grinned, and shrugged his shoulders. "You can never be too careful."

I swallowed the hard ball of fear rising from the pit of my stomach and looked past him. "This place is huge. No wonder finding missing containers is such a challenge."

"The port stretches for two miles."

I opened the Ferrari's door and lowered a Blahnik to the pavement. "Two miles?" That was a lot of port for René to search.

John offered me his free hand.

I let my fingers slot into his open palm and stood.

He led me toward a ten-foot tall fence topped with razor wire and swiped a keycard.

"Where do we find Lyman Cox?" Maybe René made some kind of mistake about the office on Canal Street. Today would be so much easier if John was one of the good guys.

"About that—" The gate clanged shut behind us.

"Yes?"

"I'm afraid he's not here."

"Where is he?" I'd play pretty and dumb as long as I could—all day if I had to.

"He's probably at Custom House."

Dammit. John wore a black hat. "Where's that?" I looked around, searching, still playing ditzy for all I was worth.

"Back on Canal Street. We passed it on our way here."

I widened my eyes. "I don't understand."

"I think you do." And he was right, I understood perfectly. John Howard wasn't just dirty. He was filthy. And I was in trouble.

I glanced back at the near-empty parking lot. One Ferrari, one Mercedes, a handful of Ford and Chevy trucks, and a black Audi R8. No people.

"Let's go." John dug his Ruger into my ribs.

"Where?"

"You want to see Smith?" He twisted Jake's name into something contemptible.

"Did you hurt him?"

"Yes."

The sound that slipped through my lips was half-sob and half-gasp. "What did you do? Is he alive?"

"He's alive and he's dying to see you."

Well, that was scary. "Why did you bring me here?" If he planned on killing me, he could have done it back at the house. Not that I wanted him killing me anywhere.

"There's a possibility Smith knows where the containers are. He won't talk when we hurt him; hurting someone he cares about might loosen him up."

My insides turned liquid and I stumbled.

John caught my arm. His fingers felt like a steel vise around the fabric of my jacket.

"How could you—"

He dug the gun farther into my ribs and propelled me forward. "Do you have any idea how much money is at stake?"

I did. I'd been to Sinaloa. I'd seen the long string of zeros at the end of the cartel's bank balances. I knew exactly how much money—and John had betrayed everything for a small portion.

The sound of a train squealing on the sidings next to the port drowned out whatever John said next. Maybe it was instructions to move faster, because he tightened his grip and yanked me forward—toward a white corrugated-metal building set on the edge of the container city.

Much as I wanted to help Jake, I didn't think things would turn out well for either one of us if I let John take me inside that building. I slowed my steps.

"Get moving."

"You try walking in these things."

We both glanced at my feet.

"Why did you have me dress up?"

"I promised the boys a treat."

I pretended fear—I widened my eyes, I gasped, I wrinkled my forehead. Truth was, I'd die before I let one of John's "boys" touch me. Unless someone was holding a gun to Jake's head. What would I do then? Submit?

The answer decided me. I was not entering that building. Absolutely, categorically not. "Where's Rose?" I demanded. "What have you done with her?" Had she been a treat for the boys?

"She's been keeping your boyfriend company."

"And Thor?"

"Who?"

"The Norse god of thunder." John didn't have Mark. Thor was out there. Somewhere. I gazed up at a huge stack of containers. This place was so huge. And Thor could be anywhere. Saving Jake and Rose was up to me. I knew it in my bones.

I knew other things. John Howard was sloppy. He hadn't searched me. I still had two guns. And I had a weapon he'd never imagined.

I leaned against the hand grasping my arm, lifted my knee, and sank four inches of stiletto into the top of his foot. At the same time, I grabbed the wrist of the hand holding the gun and jerked.

Bang!

The bullet missed me by inches.

John let go of his hold on me and swung a fist.

I anticipated the blow and bent out of his reach.

Missing me threw him off balance.

I pulled my arm back and hit him. As hard as I could. In the nose.

Blood erupted like Mount Vesuvius.

He raised his free hand to his face. The gun he pointed at the base of a container.

Now was my chance. "Drop the gun."

He didn't.

"Drop the gun or I'll shoot you."

His eyes narrowed. I could almost see the cogs in his brain spinning. How quickly could he shift the aim of his gun? How fast was I? He assessed me and the .22 I'd pulled from my waistband. He didn't believe I'd shoot him.

He lifted his gun.

I shot him in the knee.

His collapse onto the pavement was the best part of my Monday so far. I raced toward him and kicked the Ruger out of his hand.

The gun skittered across the pavement.

Then I stepped back. "Give me your wallet."

"You're robbing me?"

How much time did I have before someone came to investigate? "Give me your wallet or I'll shoot you in the other knee."

"Bitch."

I took aim.

"Okay!" He hurled the slender bit of folded leather at my feet.

I bent, withdrew the keycard for the gate, and dropped everything else to the pavement. Then I took several steps backward, scooped up his fallen gun, and ran as fast as my Blahniks allowed.

When I was out of John's sight, I changed directions.

I kept running, putting as much distance between John and myself as quickly as I could. My breath came in short pants. My feet screamed *curb shoes*! My hands shook. I ducked behind a stack of containers as big as a house and leaned my back against warm metal. I didn't have much time.

I peeked around the container stack's corner. Three men—Tall One, Small One, Wide One—milled outside the entrance to the building where Jake and Rose were being held.

Did I have it in me to shoot all three? Jake was in there. And Rose. They weren't exactly close, so I slipped the .22 back into my waistband and raised the Ruger. Its weight was unfamiliar in my sweat-slicked hand. If I shot at them, I couldn't miss. I traded the Ruger for the Glock in my purse, lifted the more familiar gun, and aimed.

My finger refused to pull the trigger. Refused. I didn't have it in me to shoot someone in cold blood.

The men glanced over their shoulders as if they were listening. Then they separated, slipping into the container city.

Someone had given them instructions.

I crouched low.

How many were left inside?

"Over here!" John's voice echoed off the metal containers followed by the sound of running. And voices. Loud, angry voices.

Note to self: start carrying duct tape in my purse. That, or shoot to kill.

I crept toward the building.

"Poppy." My name was barely a whisper.

But that whisper was enough to spike my heartbeat.

I raised my gun and turned.

Thor stood a few feet behind me.

"Where the hell have you been?" I demanded, my voice a furious rasp.

"Locked in this damned enclosure."

"How did you get in here?"

"I hopped on the back bumper of a truck. I didn't realized I'd be locked in."

"You couldn't call and tell me where you were?"

He flushed. Bright red.

"What? What happened?"

"I climbed onto some containers for a better look." He scowled at the nearest container, bright blue and glinting dully in the sunshine.

"And?" I prompted.

"They shifted. I dropped my gun and my phone. They fell between the containers."

One day, if we made it out of this, I'd tease him mercilessly. "Do they know you're here?"

"No."

I dug in my purse, then handed him John Howard's Ruger. "How many men?"

"The three outside, plus three more in the building." His forehead creased and his lips thinned. "Knox Arnaut is part of this. He's in there."

"I saw his car." Right now, I didn't care about Knox. "You're sure Jake's in there?"

"Yeah."

"Detective Langlois knows I'm here—knows I'm in trouble. He'll send officers."

"The port is a big place and Jake may not have that much time. What did you do to Howard?"

"I shot him in the knee."

Thor's teeth sparkled. "Way to maim him for life."

"Howard will send those men to look for me."

"Even if we get to Jake, we're still trapped in here."

I held up the keycard. "No, we're not."

"You can get out. Now. I'll draw them away from the fence and—"

"You really think I'd leave you to deal with six men alone?" I shook my head. "Not in a million years."

"Clear." A voice bounced off the nearest container.

"They're looking for us." I glanced back at the white building. "How do we get in there?"

Thor's answering grin was almost savage. "We go hunting."

I wasn't exactly dressed for hunting—pencil skirt and stilettos—but I was willing to try. "Where—get down!"

Thor hit the pavement as I pulled the Glock's trigger.

Wide One fell backward.

The sound of the gunshot bounced off the metal till my ears rang. I steadied myself against the container. Where were the other two?

Thor pushed himself to his knees, then his feet. "One down, five to go."

I'd killed someone.

My stomach twisted.

"C'mon—" Thor held out his hand "—we need to move. Can you run in those shoes?"

"Not fast. Not far."

"Why did you wear them?"

"Long story."

Thor peeked around the corner and motioned for me to stay back. "Federal agent! Drop your weapon."

Bang!

The first bullet hit the container well above Thor's head.

Bang!

The next bullet was closer.

Bang! Bang! Bang!

Those bullets missed wide.

Thor took aim.

Bang!

The sound of a body collapsing to the pavement shouldn't have been so sweet.

"Is he dead?" I asked.

Thor answered with a nod.

"We should go back to Howard," I whispered. "I bet the third guy is with him."

I led the way.

John Howard wasn't where I'd left him.

Instead, with his arm draped around Tall One's shoulders, he limped toward the white building.

"Stop!" If John made it to that building, he'd kill Jake. Rose too. I was sure of it.

John and Tall One didn't stop. If anything, they hobbled faster.

"Federal agent," boomed Thor. "Drop your weapons and turn around slowly."

That stopped them. For a tense few seconds, they didn't move. At all. Then Tall One bent and put his gun on the pavement. They turned. Slowly.

Then everything happened too fast.

Bang!

Tall One shot at Thor. The man had a second gun!

Bang!

Bang!

The shots from my Glock rang in my ears.

The two men sprawled across the pavement amidst growing pools of blood.

I lowered my arm and looked over my shoulder.

Thor leaned against a container and his shirt was covered in crimson.

"Where are you hit?" My voice was too high. Too fast.

"Shoulder. I'll live." He nodded toward the building. "There are three left inside."

"Okay." I took a step forward.

"Wait! I didn't mean to go after them. I meant—" he winced "—wait for backup."

"No."

"Poppy—"

"What?" I didn't want to hear about how I couldn't, how I wasn't trained, how I was a little girl playing a big man's game.

"Poppy—"

"What?" I put all my frustration into that one word.

"Be careful."

I stared at him for a few long seconds. He had faith in me despite my lack of training. He believed in me. I kissed him. A short, quick kiss that surprised us both. Then I ran to the next container block.

A single man stood in front of the white building—Billy Bouchet.

"Put down your weapon, Billy. Howard is dead, and the police are on their way."

Bang!

Billy's bullet went wide.

Dammit. Why did he have to be such an idiot? I didn't want to shoot anyone else.

Bang!

This bullet was closer.

Billy wore a black shirt. It stood out like a target against the white building. The man really did have rocks for brains.

"Billy, it's over."

Bang!

This shot hit a few feet above my head.

Bang!

Billy fell to the concrete. I felt sick.

I took a few deep breaths, then yelled, "Knox!"

"Poppy? Is that you?"

"Come out!"

"What are you doing here?"

"Come out, and bring Jake and Rose with you."

There was no response.

"I don't care if you run, Knox. I'll let you. I just want to know Jake and Rose are safe."

Thirty seconds passed.

"Knox!"

Another thirty seconds passed.

"Knox!"

Bang!

I whirled around.

Ray lay on the pavement with a bullet hole in his neck.

Thor still had one hand clasped to his shoulder. The other held the Ruger. "You don't get to kiss me like that then get yourself killed."

"Thanks."

He nodded toward the building.

Knox stood in the doorway with a gun to Jake's head. Blood had dried on one side of Jake's face and he cradled his left arm in his right.

"Let him go, Knox."

Knox's gaze searched the containers. "When I get to the car."

I looked over at Thor. "Can you check on Rose?"

He nodded. "Be careful."

"You too."

I followed Knox and Jake all the way to the parking lot.

Knox maneuvered himself next to the R8's door.

"Poppy, get out of here."

"Shut up, Jake." The man was beyond annoying. I was the only one not bleeding or running or shot and he still thought me incompetent.

Knox shoved Jake forward.

Jake fell to the ground.

Bang!

Then Knox was in his Audi, speeding out of the parking lot, fishtailing on the turn.

"Are you hit?" I cried.

"No. Are you?"

I was not. I ran to the Ferrari and slid behind the wheel.

"You can't go after him. You hit a lawnmower. You—"

I didn't wait for the rest of Jake's sentence. I sped after Knox.

I shifted gears, steered, and dug out my phone (a third hand would have been nice).

The engine growled as if thrilled to be speeding down a city street at seventy miles per hour.

I hit recent calls, then René's number. "René"

"Poppy, where are you?"

I put the phone on speaker and dropped it in my lap. "I'm following Knox Arnaut."

"Knox Arnaut?"

"Yes."

"Where exactly are you?"

I stole an eighty-miles-per-hour peek at a street sign. "Chew-pit-ew-lass."

"Where?"

"T-C-H-O-U—"

"Chop-it-tool-luss."

Everyone was a critic. "Whatever."

"What did he do? How is Arnaut involved in all this?"

"Can you just trust me?" Ninety-mile-per-hour explanations weren't my thing. "We're getting on I-10."

"What's he driving?"

"A black Audi R8."

"And you're keeping up? What are you driving?"

"A Ferrari."

René fell silent.

Knox cut between cars, blew past cars, nearly clipped cars.

And I, with my left hand in a death grip on the steering wheel and my right hand fused to the gear knob, gained on him.

A Camry slammed on its brakes and I whipped around it, so close I could see the terrorized whites of the driver's eyes.

"We're closing the exits and putting up a road block near Kenner."

Wherever that was.

Knox drove faster. We passed cars as if they were standing still.

I pulled up next to him on the left.

He glanced at me, his face a study in disbelief. How could I, a woman, drive better than he could?

Easy answer. I took driving lessons at a track after the lawn-mower incident.

Knox jerked his steering wheel to the right.

Maybe he was trying to reach the exit ramp.

He didn't make it.

Instead his car spun in circles.

He sideswiped a Prius first.

The sound of metal scraping metal was horrendous.

Then he hit a pickup truck, crushing the front of the Audi.

Finally, the R8 wedged beneath a semi-trailer.

I eased my foot off the accelerator and pressed on the brake. "He's been in an accident. It's over."

Chapter Twenty

Wearing the ugliest bridesmaid's dress in the history of ugly bridesmaids' dresses, I followed the gloriously happy Mr. and Mrs. Carter Arnaut up St. Louis Cathedral's black and white tiled aisle.

The cathedral was so full of flowers, it smelled like a garden in springtime.

The congregation was so filled with women in pastel dresses, it looked like a flower shop.

Not that I could throw any stones. The lavender ruffles on my shoulders fluttered like petals in the wind.

I smiled.

Adele was married. At last.

And Thor waited for me at the back of the cathedral. Thor, in his tuxedo, was devastating.

When I finally reached him, he brushed a kiss across my cheek. "That's some dress."

His smile, which reached to his eyes, made me a bit weak in the knees. "Isn't it?"

"You'd look beautiful in a potato sack."

Oh. Wow. I stiffened my knees. "A potato sack would be more flattering."

"Are you ready to go to the reception?"

I nodded. This dress definitely called for one of New Orleans' extra-strong cocktails.

"I'm sorry to interrupt—"

I turned around and found Detective Langlois standing behind me. He too was looking ridiculously handsome. "May I have a word?"

My surprise at seeing him must have shown on my face because he smoothed the lapels of his tuxedo, and added, "Pete Coombs invited me."

"You may have as many words as you like."

René glanced around the emptying cathedral. "I just wanted to let you know Knox Arnaut has entered a plea deal. He'll testify against Lyman Cox for a reduced sentence."

Maybe it was wrong of me, but I wanted Knox Arnaut to spend a good long time in Angola. "Have you found the drugs?"

"Our people are checking the manifests of every container at the port. We'll find them."

I had my doubts. "I'm sure you will."

"You're leaving tomorrow?"

"Right after brunch." I glanced around the near-empty nave. "Thank you for keeping my name out of everything."

"That came from Washington. Whoever you work for, the agency you can't tell me—the people running things have some juice."

Thor laughed softly.

René continued, "As far as NOPD is concerned, you're a famous-for-being-famous bridesmaid in Adele Coombs Arnaut's wedding who was unlucky enough to be at the Columns at the wrong time."

"Sounds about right."

René huffed. "One helluva cover."

"That's what my boss says." My gaze swept the altar and the empty pews. No one was paying the slightest bit of attention to us. "What did Knox tell you?"

"Lyman Cox has been working with smugglers for years, then Vic Klein came along and Cox got greedy."

"How greedy?"

René's answering smile was cynical. "Cox decided to make one last big payday then disappear."

"He stole Klein's drugs."

René nodded. "So to speak. They're still at the port. Somewhere."

"What about Hubbard?" asked Thor.

"Mason Hubbard was something of a hacker. He switched the tracking numbers for Cox."

"But he gave him the wrong numbers?"

"He was also an opportunist. Without the correct tracking numbers, Cox couldn't find the drugs. Without the drugs, Cox betrayed the Sinaloans for nothing." René rubbed his chin. "Mason wanted a payout before he'd tell Cox where the containers were."

"What did Cox tell the Sinaloans?" I asked.

René glanced around the nave. "He told them Mason had hidden them. When Mason realized the Sinaloans might come for him, he went to the District Attorney's office."

"And he talked to Knox?"

"Smart girl." Somehow, when René said it, it didn't sound patronizing. "Meanwhile, the Sinaloans didn't realize how hard it would be to find the drugs without the tracking numbers, they just wanted the man who'd stolen from them dead."

"So they blew up a building?" Why was I surprised? I knew how vicious the cartel could be.

"Cox couldn't have Mason talking to the Sinaloans. Not when he might tell them who was really behind the theft of their drugs. Nor could he risk having Hubbard talk to anyone else in the DA's office." Rene's scowl reached all the way to his hairline.

"Cox didn't realize Hubbard had also gone to the DEA," said Thor.

"Not at first." Somehow, René's scowl deepened. "Not until Cox's dirty DEA agent, John Howard, told him."

"So it was Cox's people—John Howard and his men—who shot up the Tiger's Eye?" All those innocent people—their panicked screams still sounded in my ears.

"Bingo."

"It all made sense. Thank you for telling me." I smiled up at René.

Thor's hand closed on my elbow. "We should probably get going."

"Will we see you at the reception, René?"

"Count on it." He shot a quick glance at Thor. "Save me a dance?"

Thor grumbled about local police officers for the duration of our drive to the country club.

ADELE AND CARTER dancing their first dance brought tears to my eyes.

And to Pete Coombs's eyes as well. He stood next to me beaming at his daughter and the man she married. As the song closed, he side-eyed me. "I made a few calls to some friends in Washington."

"Oh?"

"The first cousin of the man my daughter's marrying gets

arrested a few days before the wedding—what man wouldn't make a few calls?"

Lots of men wouldn't. Not everyone enjoyed Pete's influence. I looked at up him. "I'm sorry about everything, Pete."

"Nah, none of this was your fault."

"I nearly spoiled Adele's wedding."

"Sugar, a member of Carter's extended family did something illegal. It was better to know before the I do's."

"I suppose you're right."

"Besides, now we know everything."

"Everything?"

"Heck, I even know Carter's secret."

"What is it?"

"Carter went to juvenile detention."

"Carter?" I couldn't believe it.

"Apparently Knox, who's a year older than Carter, was dealing pot. Carter took the fall for him."

"And no one knew?"

"No one outside the Arnaut family. Not until—"

I thought back to the party where I'd seen Quint Arnaut and John Howard deep in conversation. "Not until John Howard somehow found out."

"No flies on you."

"Was Howard blackmailing Quint?"

"I don't know. And Quint isn't saying."

Pete looked around the crowded ballroom. "That boyfriend of yours needs saving."

I followed his gaze.

Thor was pinned between the bar and four pretty women.

"Are you going to save him?"

"He's tougher than he looks. He can handle it."

Pete Coombs smiled and extended his hand. "Poppy, it's been a pleasure. You come visit anytime."

I approached the bar and extended my hand to Thor. "Dance with me?"

The question earned me four scathing looks but Thor grabbed my hand and led me to the dance floor.

"So—" his hand warmed the small of my back "—it's over."

"Looks like it." I smiled up at him. "I have a question."

"Shoot."

"That tail from the airport. Who was following you?"

"That was about the case I'm working in Houston. Apparently I was made. Someone followed me in Texas." His face darkened. "They must have been good, because I never saw them. At any rate, they called an associate in New Orleans when they saw where my plane was headed. That's who followed me."

"How do you know?"

"An arrest was made."

"Without you?"

"Yes."

"But it was your case!"

"I was here."

Oh. I smiled up at him. "I'm glad you were here."

He smiled back. "Me, too."

"Can you tell me about the case in Texas?"

"Nope."

Mr. Brown loved his secrets. I wrinkled my nose. "I guess we'd better just dance."

We danced, we drank, we ate, and at midnight, Thor whispered in my ear, "We've got to go."

"Go? Where?"

"It's a surprise."

He drove me to a modest building on Canal Street.

"Chickie Wah Wah? I think we're overdressed."

"It's a special show."

"You're very mysterious."

"Thank you."

He parked James's Ferrari—I was going to miss that car—and escorted me to the door.

The bouncer—ubiquitous black tee-shirt—had a list. "Name?"

"Mark Stone."

The man at the door waved us through.

Inside, Rose O'Leary stood at the front of a small stage and sang, "Angel from Montgomery."

Jake and Mama Vielle sat directly in front of her—at a table with two empty chairs.

Jake looked at me with a smirk on his face. "Nice dress."

"You know when we were at the hospital, and the doctors set your arm, and removed the bullet, and stitched you up, and I told you I was glad you were alive?"

"Yes."

"I take it back."

He pushed out a chair.

I ignored it and sat next to Mama Vielle. "How are you feeling?"

She patted my hand. "I'll be right as rain in no time."

"I'm glad to hear that."

"You still got that hoodoo I gave you?"

"I do."

"You keep it with you. Trouble ain't done with you yet."

I'd signed up for trouble. "I'll keep it. I promise."

"How was the wedding?" asked Jake.

"Beautiful." I ran the rolled edge of a ruffle between my fingers. "I am done with weddings for a long, long time." I had training to complete, and neither Mia nor André, my best friends, were even dating anyone.

"You sure about that?" Jake's grin widened.

"What do you know that I don't?"

Jake pushed his phone across the table to me, and I looked at a picture of my mother. The caption below her face told me Chariss Carlton was engaged to Russian billionaire Yurgi Prokorhov.

"I'm going to need a drink." A strong one. I liked Yurgi but —but Chariss had only known him a short time. I swiveled my head and looked for a server.

My phone rang.

I stared at the screen for a few seconds before answering. "Hello, Chariss. Something you want to tell me?"

"Thank God I reached you." Chariss's voice was high and breathy. "You've got to come to London. Right away."

"I have something on my calendar." I was going for training; she'd have to plan her wedding without me.

"Poppy, you don't understand—"

"I do. You're getting married. Best wishes."

"No! You don't understand. Yurgi's been kidnapped. I need you to come to London. Now." She waited a few seconds, then added, "Please."

Also by Julie Mulhern

The Poppy Fields Adventures

Fields' Guide to Abduction

Fields Guide to Assassins

Fields Guide to Voodoo

The Country Club Murders

The Deep End

Guaranteed to Bleed

Clouds in My Coffee

Send in the Clowns

Watching the Detectives

Cold as Ice

Shadow Dancing

Back Stabbers

Let's keep in touch!

About the Author

Julie Mulhern is the USA Today bestselling author of The Country Club Murders and the Poppy Fields Adventures.

She is a Kansas City native who grew up on a steady diet of Agatha Christie. She spends her spare time whipping up gourmet meals for her family, working out at the gym and finding new ways to keep her house spotlessly clean--and she's got an active imagination. Truth is--she's an expert at calling for take-out, she grumbles about walking the dog and the dust bunnies under the bed have grown into dust lions.

Made in the USA
San Bernardino, CA
09 June 2019